To the Contrary

To the Contrary: Stories by AA Navis

For further information, contact:
The Lontar Foundation
Jl. Danau Laut Tawar No. 53
Jakarta 10210 Indonesia
www.lontar.org

Publication of this title in the Modern Library of Indonesia series
has been made possible by the generous assistance of The Ford Foundation

Template design by DesignLab; layout and cover by Cyprianus Jaya Napiun
Cover illustration: *Suami Istri* (Husband and Wife) by H Widayat;
Image courtesy of the OHD Museum of Modern & Contemporary Indonesian Art

ISBN No. 978-602-6978-93-6

MODERN LIBRARY OF INDONESIA

AA NAVIS

To the Contrary
Stories

translated by
Kevin W Fogg and Matthew GB Woolgar

with an introduction by
Kevin W Fogg

Jakarta, Indonesia

Contents

AA Navis: The Man and His Work

A A Navis was born in the Javanese quarter of the West Sumatran city of Padang Panjang on 17 November 1924, the oldest of eleven children (sixteen if counting half-siblings by his father). "Navis" was actually his father's name; his father was part of the small community of Javanese who had moved there to the heartlands of the matrilineal Minangkabau people. His personal name, Ali Akbar, was much more classically Minang. Thus, his full name shows that from the beginning he was a bit betwixt and between.

The era he was born into was also rather betwixt and between. The 1920s and 1930s, as he grew up, were both the peak and the twilight of the Dutch colonial era in the Netherlands East Indies, soon to become Indonesia. The Minangkabau heartlands experienced this time with more political intensity than most regions, and several Minang leaders one generation older than Navis went on to become pioneers of nationalism with many different political stripes. Rapid modernization was happening all around: the Dutch had vastly improved educational opportunities for Minangkabau youth in the decades earlier, and in response Islamic and other native schools sprung up to provide indigenous alternatives to colonial modernity. These schools taught modern subjects like mathematics, bookkeeping, and Dutch language, but they also tried to instill Indonesian pride and Islamic beliefs in their students.

AA Navis attended one of these native schools, called I.N.S. (Indonesisch Nederlandsche School) Kayutanam, a short train ride from his hometown in the highlands down towards the coast, through the plunging Batang Anai gorge (the same journey that is a central feature in the story "The Water Buffalo Asks the Cart"). This school was led by the famous Minangkabau educator M. Sjafei, a product of Dutch schools who collaborated with the local railway workers union to establish a school for creating modern, educated Indonesians in a nationalist mold—not just for Dutch colonial purposes. Navis studied there for eleven years, until his formal education was cut off by the Japanese invasion.

As a young boy, Navis was smaller than his classmates, which apparently often led to him getting in fights at school and on his way home from school. This made him scrappy and contributed to the cynicism that comes through sharply in his writings. It also taught him determination, which he later credited for his success as an author.

I.N.S. Kayutanam was to remain one of the mainstays of Navis's entire life. In the 1970s and again in the 1990s he was chair of the school's board, and through the 1980s he retained a room on its campus to write and read. Occasionally he would spend longer stretches of time there to focus on work. When Navis went on the pilgrimage to Mecca, the prosperity of the school was one of three things he prayed for in the grand mosque, Islam's holiest place.

The education Navis received at I.N.S. Kayutanam was varied. He studied traditional subjects like mathematics and civics, but there were also plenty of opportunities to study the arts. Navis was not only interested in writing fiction; he also experimented with sculpture and music (he played the flute), and worked designing posters to earn some extra income while in school. This might also be the reason why many of the characters that appeared in his later stories were artists of other kinds, such as the aspiring sculptor in

"Maria"— they were reflections of other directions he believed his life could have gone.

As a teenager, Navis lived through the most tumultuous time in modern Indonesian history: the Japanese occupation and Indonesian Revolution. These were times of extremes, and some of their excesses became topics for his later fiction, including "Third Class Passenger." He was also an active supporter of the independence movement; his brother reported that most of the motivational banners promoting Indonesian independence around the provincial capital (at that time, Bukittinggi, where Navis moved in 1945) were painted by Navis in his home. He also contributed to the programming on Indonesian radio during the Revolution.

The mid-1950s brought AA Navis his major literary breakthrough. The short story "The Collapse of Our Prayer House," first seen in a national literary magazine in 1955 and then published in a collection of six stories by Navis in 1956, was hailed as insightful, incisive, and relevant for newly independent Indonesia. The collection of short stories under this title has been reprinted at least eleven times, with additional stories added in later versions. The original six stories were written more quickly than almost any other literary works that Navis published later, but their moral force was still undeniable. The acclaim for his short fiction, and the story "The Collapse of Our Prayer House" in particular, made AA Navis a leading name in Indonesian literature from the 1950s.

In 1957, Navis married a woman he had met through his radio work, Aksari Yasin (their romance—and relative heights—mirrored the characters in "An Ideal Match"). They were blessed with eight children. Throughout their life together, Aksari held regular work as a teacher and brought home a steady salary (and, later, a steady pension). Navis dedicated himself to writing, which meant getting paid only when he was able to sell a story or complete a book.

In this arrangement, where the wife was the financial rock of the family, it is unsurprising that Navis frequently wrote about gender roles, relationships, and women's issues. This might also reflect the particularly prominent role of women in Minangkabau society, which is matrilineal. According to the family, Aksari was also always Navis's first reader for his drafts, and she provided very real feedback, not just praise.

In the 1950s, Navis tried working for the provincial office of the Ministry of Culture, but he disliked it so much that he quit after three years. During the unsuccessful regional rebellion from 1958 to 1961, Navis took his young family to the rural area around Lake Maninjau and remained unaligned in the conflict, although several of his younger brothers did pick up arms. Although driven out of the city, he remained active writing, producing many of the stories that appeared in his second and third collections. After the dust settled, the family eventually relocated to the new provincial capital in Padang, where he was based for the rest of his life.

In the 1970s, he had regular work as the editor of a newspaper, in addition to his ongoing relationship with his old school. This period was also when he entered a different kind of government service, serving eleven years in the provincial legislature from 1971 to 1982, representing the government party Golkar. Navis reported hating the morass of the faux legislative process in authoritarian Indonesia. Apparently, the stress of serving gave him hemorrhoids the entire time he was in the provincial assembly, with the problem clearing up shortly after he relinquished that post. A few years after he left government service, he published the bitingly critical allegory "The Cats" and the cynical story "The Old Order," which indict the inefficiency, corruption, and groupthink of bureaucracy, albeit in a slightly indirect way.

In the middle of his career, Navis had suggested that the topics of his short stories might also have been the result of the space available to him in New Order Indonesia. He wrote, "I want to write about the military affairs that have happened to us in all this time. I also want to write about the awakening of the Muslim community. But my desires were always blocked because I know that I will not be able to find a publisher who would want to publish it. If I wrote it all, I would just put it on the shelf, to be eaten by termites, and I guess I would have done work that was a waste."

The 1990s brought new productivity, as Navis was able to focus on writing again. He published several works that had been written earlier but remained unpublished, and he also wrote new stories with commentary on the times. Even "Chatting at Eid," a contemplative story written when Navis was seventy-seven years old, has his thinly-veiled reaction to the terrorist attacks in the name of Islam in 2001. In his semi-retirement, Navis not only wrote and supported his old school, but he also taught at Andalas University in Padang and spoke at many national and international seminars.

In addition to his literary heft, his impact on the Muslim community was also clear. The great Indonesian historian Taufik Abdullah, also ethnically Minangkabau, called Navis "a reformer in the religious sense," because his writing caused Muslims to think about and probe their own religious positions. Abdurrahman Wahid, popularly known as Gus Dur, a golden boy of the country's largest Islamic organization Nahdlatul Ulama (NU) and later Indonesia's fourth president (1999–2000), was reportedly deeply affected by the story "The Collapse of Our Prayer House." The cynical take on public piety was not without controversy, and the scandals and sin in other stories also ruffled feathers. Navis was briefly seen as leftist or even Communist, so in the early 1960s he wrote a novel and took public stands to assert his belief in "Islam as against humanism"—a position that was somewhat dangerous at the time. By the 1980s, he had an established reputation for the

Islamic influence on his literary production, and for this reason the Indonesian Ministry of Religion paid for his pilgrimage to Mecca in hopes of more religiously inclined literary works.

In terms of his style, the great Indonesian literary critic HB Jassin called him "cynical but funny." Much like the famous American short story author O. Henry, Navis often put a surprising twist at the end of his tales, which would both provide a kind of humorous turn to amuse readers and a biting critique of the situation. This is true in both his light-hearted and more serious stories, as can be seen in "The Two of Them" and "An Interview." Allegory was also a particular strength. A story like "Marah, Who Endured," published in 1998, might be read as a veiled condemnation of the violence along ethnic lines in political transition out of authoritarianism.

Navis also had an impressive ability to write moral ambiguity. This is not to say that none of his stories had clear moral messages; reading "The Water Buffalo Asks the Cart" will quickly prove otherwise. However, in many short stories, such as "A Wedding," Navis made compelling arguments in favor of two, contradictory moral positions. He also exercised restraint in these stories from spoon-feeding lessons to his readers. Instead, the moral ambiguity of certain stories was used to prompt thought.

Navis told an interviewer in the 1990s "I do not write for stupid people;" he expected his readers to be at least as smart as he was (a very high bar). This meant that he could put the task of analysis or moral reflection on the readers consistently. He was less consistent in the subjects or tone of his fiction. His short stories ranged from pitifully tragic, such as "Pride and Joy," to deeply skeptical of modern "progress," as in "The Foreigners," to haunting social commentary, like "Shadows." The only element that seemed constant across his fiction was a somewhat insistent Minangkabau—not Javanese, not pan-Indonesian—perspective. Even his autobiography, published in 1994, was pointedly subtitled *Satiris dan Suara Kritis dari Daerah* (Satirist and Critical Voice from the Regions), i.e., not the national capital. This was also reflected in his use of some Sumatran-inflected words and in his invocation of ethnic folktales, as seen in "A Hero's Tale".

Short stories, although Navis's most famous and even favorite artistic medium, were not his only output. He also wrote several novels; some published serially in newspapers or magazines. The most famous of these was *Kemarau* (Drought), first published in 1967, which integrated the short story "Comings and Goings." Other themes in his novels included campus and education, family relations, and Minangkabau city life. Navis also dabbled in poetry (including a collection published in 1975) and radio-plays, although these never won him as much acclaim as his short fiction.

Navis also wrote non-fiction books on topics of interest or relevance to him. The most famous of these books were treatises on his native Minangkabau people, such as *Alam Terkembang Jadi Guru: Adat dan Kebudayaan Minangkabau* (1984) (The Living World as Teacher: Traditions and Culture of the Minangkabau), which is still in print today. Another major non-fiction work was a labor of love for his old teacher and school at I.N.S. Kayutanam: *Filsafat dan Strategi Pendidikan M. Sjafei* (1996) (The Educational Philosophy and Strategy of M. Sjafei). He was also active writing in the press, especially the newspapers of West Sumatra where he had worked for some time as a newspaper editor. The subjects ranged from literature and culture to religion, education and current affairs. Many of these articles were collected in the volume *Yang Berjalan Sepanjang Jalan* (The One who Walks to the End of the Road), published in 1999.

As seen in Navis's non-fiction, he functioned as a cultural expert, even a living cultural treasure, for the Minangkabau people. It was in this role as a cultural expert that Navis collected three volumes of Minangkabau folktales, published in the 1990s, which led to an award from UNESCO in 1999. Amid his love of his people, though, he also thought very critically about his own culture: the place of Islam, the value of tradition, the impact of modernity and the Indonesian state. As much as he loved Minangkabau culture, he was never shy about criticizing his own people or rejecting traditions that were holding them back.

Although the most famous work in his whole career was his earliest, for which he won a prize from the magazine *Kisah* for short story of the year in 1955, his other short stories have also been acclaimed. In 1975, he won a Dutch prize for his story "An Ideal Match," and in 1979 Indonesia's leading women's magazine, *Femina*, gave an award to his short story "A Wedding." In 1992, the Association of Southeast Asian Nations (ASEAN) honored him at a meeting in Bangkok for his short-story collection *Hujan Panas dan Kabut Musim* (Hot Rain and Seasonal Fog). In that same year he received a literary award from the Indonesian Ministry of Education and Culture. The greatest sign of his importance, though, has been the continued republication of his works, including the posthumous, authoritative *Antologi Lengkap Cerpen* (Complete Anthology of Short Stories) in 2005, from which this volume pulls its selections.

Navis died on 23 March 2003 in the West Sumatran capital city, Padang. At his funeral, a former Minister of Religion, Tarmizi Taher, and the head of Indonesia's second-largest Islamic organization Muhammadiyah, M. Syafi'i Maarif, both attended. His legacy lives on, with several of his unpublished writings on Minangkabau culture and history being edited together by a local professor in 2017. Even now, some sixty years after he first wrote short fiction, Navis's satirical and critical voice remains as incisive and necessary as ever.

Sources

Abdullah, Taufik. *Schools and Politics: The Kaum Muda Movement in West Sumatra (1927-1933)*; Ithaca, NY: Cornell Modern Indonesia Project, 1971.

Adilla, Ivan. *AA Navis: Karya dan Dunianya*; Jakarta: Grasindo, 2003.

Adilla, Ivan. "AA Navis dalam Arena Kesusasteraan Indonesia," doctoral dissertation, Fakultas Ilmu Budaya, Universitas Gajah Mada, 2015.

Erneste, Pamusuk. "Kenangan pada AA Navis: Catatan Lepas Seorang Editor," *Mata Baca*, vol. 1, no. 9 (Mei 2003).

Fogg, Kevin W. Interview with Anas Nafis, Padang, 10 March 2006.

Fogg, Kevin W. Interview with Gemala Rasti, Padang, 24 January 2017.

Navis, AA. In *Proses Kreatif: Mengapa dan Bagaimana Saya Mengarang*, Pamusuk Eneste, ed., vol. II; Jakarta: Gramedia, 1982.

Navis, AA. *Alam Terkembang Jadi Guru: Adat dan Kebudayaan Minangkabau*; Jakarta: Grafti Pers, 1984.

Navis, AA. *Otobiograf AA Navis: Satiris dan Suara Kritis dari Daerah*, Abrar Yusra, ed.; Jakarta: Gramedia, 1994.

Navis, AA. *Filsafat dan Strategi Pendidikan M. Sjafei: Ruang Pendidik INS Kayutanam*; Jakarta: Grasindo, 1996.

Navis, AA. *Yang Berjalan Sepanjang Jalan: Kumpulan Karangan Pilihan*; Jakarta: Grasindo, 1999.

Navis, AA. "AA Navis: Suara Satiris dari Daerah," a film in the Lontar Foundation series On the Record; Jakarta: Lontar, 2004.

Navis, AA. *Antologi Lengkap Cerpen*; Jakarta: Kompas, 2005.

Phillips, Nigel. "Two West Sumatran Writers: AA Navis and

Nurdin Yakub," in Jeremy HCS Davidson and Helen Cordell, eds., *The Short Story in South East Asia: Aspects of a Genre*; London: SOAS, 1982.

Zed, Mestika, ed. *Pemikiran Minangkabau: Catatan Budaya AA Navis*; Bandung: Angkasa, 2017.

The Collapse of Our Prayer House

I f you had come to my hometown a few years ago by bus, you would have stopped near the market. If you had walked along the main road headed west, about a kilometer down the way from the market, you would have reached my neighborhood. At the fifth intersection, if you turned onto the narrowest street, at the end you would have found an old prayer house. In front of it was a fishpond, where the water flowed through four taps for bathing.

And on the field to the right of the prayer house you would have met an old man who usually sat there, his age and his piety in prayers plain for all to see. For years he acted as the *garin*, or caretaker of the prayer house. Folks called him Grandpa.

Grandpa didn't get anything for being caretaker of the prayer house. He lived on the charity collected once a week during Friday prayers. Every six months he would get one fourth of the harvest of goldfish when they drained the fishpond. And once a year people would give their offerings for the end of the fasting month to him. But as a *garin* he wasn't particularly well-known. He was better known as a knife-sharpener. It was because he was so skillful at it. Folks would come ask him for help, but he never asked for anything in return. Women would come asking him to sharpen a knife or scissors and give him chili sauce in return. Men would come asking for help, and give him back some smokes, sometimes money. But what he most often received in return was an expression of thanks and a bit of a smile.

But now Grandpa is no more. He's already passed away. And now the prayer house has no caretaker. It's gotten to the point where kids use it as a place to play, playing whatever games they like. Women who are out of firewood come all the time to pull off some of the siding or flooring at night.

If you came now, you would meet a picture that impresses on you a kind of sanctity that has collapsed. And that process of collapse keeps getting faster and faster as time passes. As fast as the kids run around inside there, as fast as women pull apart its planks. And, the greatest sign of mankind's idiocy in our times, no one wants to take care of something that no longer has a caretaker.

And behind this collapse is a tale whose truth cannot be disputed. This is the story.

One day I came to give Grandpa a little money. Usually Grandpa was happy to receive me, because I liked to give him money. But this time Grandpa was in a mood. He sat all the way in the corner, with his knees propping up his arms and chin. He stared straight ahead full of melancholy, as though there was something terrorizing his thoughts. A little milk jar filled with coconut oil, a fine whetting stone, some leather soles, and a pretty old knife were scattered around Grandpa's feet. I had never seen Grandpa in such low spirits, and he had never let my greeting go unanswered like he did that time. So, I sat next to him and I patted the knife. And I asked Grandpa: "Whose knife is it, Gramps?"

"Ajo Sidi."

"Ajo Sidi?"

Grandpa said nothing. But I remembered Ajo Sidi, that loudmouth. It had been a long time since I had seen him. And I wanted to see him again. I enjoyed hearing him spin tales. Ajo Sidi could enthrall folks with his strange made-up stories all day long. But this rarely happened, because he was always so busy with his work. As the neighborhood loudmouth, his greatest success was when all the characters woven into his stories became stand-ins for people he could insult, and when his story became the last word on them. There were actually some folks around my neighborhood who acted exactly like the characters in his stories. When he once regaled us with a story about a toad, it was no coincidence that there was a fellow trying to become a village headman who acted exactly like that toad, and from then on we always called him the toad headman.

Suddenly I was reminded of Grandpa and his dealings with Ajo Sidi. Did Ajo Sidi tell some biting story about Grandpa? And was that biting story what made Grandpa so melancholy? I wanted to know. So I asked Grandpa: "What was the story, Gramps?"

"Whose story?"

"Ajo Sidi's."

"No manners at all," Grandpa answered.

"What do you mean?"

"Hopefully the razor I'm sharpening here will slit his throat."

"Grandpa, are you angry?"

"Angry? Yeah, I would be if I were still young, but I'm already an old man. Old men have to put up with all kinds of things. It's been a long time since I've gotten angry over things. I'm afraid that it would spoil my faith, and spoil my devotions. I've been doing good for so long, doing my prayers, faithful to God. For so long I've surrendered myself to Him. And God blesses those who are patient and faithful."

I wanted to know what the story was from Ajo Sidi, the story that had clouded Grandpa's thoughts almost entirely. I asked Grandpa again: "How did the story go, Gramps?"

But Grandpa was silent. Maybe his heart was too heavy to repeat the story. After I had asked over and over, he asked me back, "You know me pretty well, right? Since you were small I've been here. Since I was young, right? You know everything I've done, right? Have I done anything damnable? Does God condemn all my work?"

But I didn't need to answer him any further. Because I knew, if Grandpa opened his mouth again, he wouldn't be able to contain himself anymore. I left Grandpa to face his own questions.

"Since I was young I've been here, right? I didn't have a wife, kids, a family like other people, you know? I didn't imagine I would spend life alone. I didn't seek after wealth, build a house. My whole life, heart and soul, I have surrendered myself to God Almighty, blessed be His name. I have not made other folks' lives more difficult. I wouldn't kill a fly. But now I am called a damned man. Fodder for hellfire. Is God angry if this is all that I've done, do you think? Will I be damned by Him if all my life I have served Him? I never thought about my future, because I firmly believed that God exists and would show His grace and mercy to those of His people who were faithful. I got up early in the morning. I did my ablutions. I hit the mosque-drum to wake up mankind from their slumber, so they could kneel before Him. I prayed at every hour. I praised Him. I read His scriptures. 'Thank the Lord,' I would say if I were surprised. 'Praise the Lord,' I would say if I was in awe. What have I done wrong in my work? But now, I am called a damned man."

When Grandpa was quiet for a good while, I threw out a question: "He said that's how it is for you, Grandpa?"

"He didn't say I was damned. But that's about what he meant."

And I watched Grandpa's eyes well up. Mine welled up in return. In my heart I reproached Ajo Sidi. But I still wanted to know what Ajo Sidi's story was that had pummeled Grandpa's heart so bad. And my desire to know made me nosy enough to ask. And in the end Grandpa told the story, too.

ᘓ

One fateful day, Ajo Sidi said to start off, in the great hereafter the Lord God was judging all people who had already been called home. The angels stood at attention by His side. In their hands they held lists of the sins and good deeds of mankind. The people being judged were legion. Remember that there had been war all over the place. And among those people being judged there was a man who had been called on earth by the name Haji Saleh. Haji Saleh just smiled, because he was so confident that he would be sent to heaven. He had both his hands on his hips and thrust out his chest and leaned his head back a bit. When he saw the people sent to hell, his lips sketched a self-righteous smile. When he saw people sent to heaven, he waved at them, as if to say, "See you soon." It seemed unending, the line of people was so long. When the front of the line passed through, more were added to the back. And God judged them with all His qualities.

Finally, it came Haji Saleh's turn. While smiling proudly he paid homage to God. Then God asked his first question.

"And you are?"

"I am Saleh. But because I have made the pilgrimage to Mecca, I am called Haji Saleh."

"I did not ask your name. Your name is unnecessary. Names are only for while you are on earth."

"Yes, my Lord."

"What did you do whilst on earth?"

"I worshipped You always, Lord."

"Besides that?"

"Every day, every night, even at every moment I would speak Your name."

"Besides that?"

"All of the things You prohibited, I stopped, O my Lord. I never did evil, despite the fact that the whole world was full of sins marshaled by the accursed devil."

"Besides that?"

"Yes, my Lord, I had no other work besides the duty of worshipping You. Why, in Your grace, when I was sick Your name was the one thing on my lips. And I always prayed, prayed for Your humility to enlighten Your people."

"Besides that?"

Haji Saleh had no other answer. He had already told God everything that he had done. But he knew that God's question was not just for the sake of asking, there must be something else that he had not said. But in his view, he had already told God everything. He knew of nothing else that he should say. He was pensive and bowed his head. The fires of hell suddenly blew their heat towards Haji Saleh's body. And he cried. But every tear that flowed down was dried right up by hell's hot flames.

"Anything besides that?" asked God.

"Your servant has already told You everything, O God the All in All, the Gracious and Merciful, the Just and Omniscient." Haji Saleh, who was already prostrate, tried every strategy to humble himself and praise God with the hope that God would be kind to him and not ask him the wrong thing.

But God asked him again: "Is there nothing besides that?"

"Oh, oh, oohhh, umm, my Lord. I always read Your Scriptures."

"Besides that?"

"I have already told You everything, O my Lord. But if there is something I have forgotten to say, I am grateful because You, Lord, are the Omniscient One."

"Truly is there nothing more that you have done on earth besides what you have just said?"

"Yes, that is all, my Lord."

"Go in."

And the angels with their might flung Haji Saleh into hell. Haji Saleh did not understand why he was carried to hell. He did not understand what God wanted from him, and he believed God could not be mistaken.

How astonished Haji Saleh was, because in hell he found many of his friends on earth burnt to a crisp, moaning in agony. Even more than before, he did not understand his own situation, because all the people he saw in hell were no less in their devotions than he himself. There was even one man who had been to Mecca fourteen times and had the title of Sheikh to boot. Then Haji Saleh drew close to them, and asked them why they were all sent to hell. But like Haji Saleh, those people did not understand it either.

"What's going on with this God of ours?" said Haji Saleh after that. "Did He not instruct us to be observant in our devotions, strong in our faith? And we did all of that, throughout our lives. But now He has sent us to hell."

"Yes, we're also surprised. Look, there are people from the same country as us, and they weren't lacking at all in their observance of devotions," said one of the people among them.

"This is unjust," said Haji Saleh.

"Truly, this is unjust," said the people.

"In this case, we have to demand the witness of our misdeeds."

"We must remind God, just in case He was mistaken in sending us to hell."

"Right. Right. Right." Cries rose up, agreeing with Haji Saleh.

"If God does not want to admit to His mistake, what then?" asked a shrill voice among the large crowd of people.

"We will protest. We will petition," said Haji Saleh.

"Will we start a revolution, too?" asked another voice, who it seemed on earth had been the leader of a revolutionary movement.

"That depends on the circumstances," said Haji Saleh. "The important thing, for now, is that we go demonstrate before God."

"Sounds great. In the world, we were able to accomplish so much using demonstrations," a voice chimed in.

"We agree. We agree. We agree," they cried in unison.

Then they set out, all together, to face God.

And God asked, "What do you all want?"

Haji Saleh, who had become the leader and spokesperson, stepped out to the front. And with a rising voice and a beautiful rhythm, he began his speech: "O, our God the Greatest. We who come before You are Your people who were most observant in our devotions, who were most observant in praising You. We here are the people who always called on Your name, praised Your greatness, spread news of Your just nature, and more besides that. Your scriptures we memorized by heart. We wavered not the tiniest bit in reading them. However, our God the Omnipotent, after You had called us unto You, You sent us into hell. So before something undesirable happens, we have come here, in the name of the people who have loved You, and we are calling for the punishments that You delivered on our heads to be reconsidered, and for You to send us into heaven just as You have promised in Your Scriptures."

"Where did you all live when on earth?" asked God.

"We are Your people who lived in Indonesia, my Lord."

"Oh, in that country whose land is so fertile?"

"Yes, that is correct, Lord."

"Whose land is so incredibly rich, filled with metals, oil, and all kinds of things to be mined, right?"

"Right. Right. Right, our Lord. That is our country." They began to answer at the same time. Because the dawn of happiness was beginning to be seen across their faces again. And they firmly believed now that God had been mistaken in sending them to the punishment of hell.

"In the country that is so fertile, such that plants grow without being planted?"

"Right. Right. Right. That is our country."

"The country where the inhabitants themselves are impoverished?"

"Yes. Yes. Yes. That is our country."

"The country that was enslaved by other people for so long?"

"Yes, my Lord. The colonizers were so awful, my Lord."

"And the fruit of your land, they were the ones who collected it up and carried it off to their country, right?"

"Right, my Lord. To the point where we did not get anything at all. They were so awful."

"The country that is always a mess, to the point where you always fight among yourselves, meanwhile the fruit of your land is collected up and taken off by other people, right?"

"Right, my Lord. But we do not care at all about questions of worldly possessions. The important thing for us is to praise and worship You."

"You are willing to remain impoverished, right?"

"Right. We are very willing, my Lord."

"Because of your willingness, your offspring remain impoverished, right?"

"Even if our offspring are impoverished, they are all still very good at reciting the scriptures. They have memorized Your scriptures by heart."

"But what is said in the scriptures did not really pierce any of your hearts, did it?"

"It did, my Lord."

"If it did, why are you allowing yourselves to remain impoverished, even such that your offspring are all destitute? Meanwhile, your possessions you let someone else carry off for their own offspring. And you prefer to fight among yourselves, trick each other, oppress each other. I gave you a country that was so rich, but you were lazy. You preferred to just do your devotions, because devotions don't make you break a sweat, devotions don't weigh down your bones. All the while I had called on you all to do good deeds in addition to devotions. How can you do good deeds if you are poor? You thought I liked praise, would get drunk off your worship, so that you did no work except just to praise and worship Me. No. You all should be sent to hell. Hark, Angels, expel these people from this place and send them back into hell. Place them in the brimstone."

The color drained from all their faces and they were not brave enough to speak a word. They knew now the path that God had wanted for them on earth. But Haji Saleh wanted to be sure whether what he'd done on earth was right or wrong. But he was not brave enough to ask God directly. He asked one of the angels escorting them.

"Was it wrong in your opinion if we praised God on earth?" asked Haji Saleh.

"No. You were wrong because you focused too much on your own self. You were so afraid to be sent to hell, and because of that you were observant in your prayers. But you forgot the lives of your own wife and children, so they were left topsy-turvy all that time. This was your greatest wrong, you were too egotistical. Even though you were on earth in a community and all of you were brothers, you still did not care about the others at all."

ᔆ

That was Ajo Sidi's story that I heard from Grandpa. The story that clouded his mind.

The next day, when I wanted to come out of the house in the morning, my wife asked if I was going to go and pay my respects.

"Who was it who died?" I asked in shock.

"Grandpa."

"Grandpa?"

"Yes. This morning at dawn Grandpa died in the most terrible circumstances in the prayer house. He slit his own throat with a razor."

"Sweet heavens. Ajo Sidi is to blame," I said, quickly leaving behind my wife who was totally aghast.

I sought out Ajo Sidi at his house. But I was only able to find his wife. So I asked her.

"He's already gone," answered Ajo Sidi's wife.

"Doesn't he know that Grandpa died?"

"He knows. And he left instructions to buy a seven-layer burial shroud for Grandpa."

"And now?" I asked, absolutely incredulous to hearthat though this whole incident was whipped up by Ajo Sidi, he didn't show a shred of responsibility. "Where has he gone now?"

"To work."

"Work?" I asked, hollowly repeating her.

"Yes. He's gone to work."

Maria

The water of the Antokan River that flows swiftly into the Indian Ocean makes a thundering sound in the place where I'm standing now. It does not stop flowing from its source, Lake Maninjau, down to the Indian Ocean. In the rebellion years of the early 1960s, many people died, swept away by the two sides fighting each other. One of these people was Maria, my friend.

03

The first time I saw her, the word "different" was carved in my heart. The second time, it was the words "a different kind of different." Even now I can still feel the place where those words are carved. That first time, I was walking in the evening with my friend Cok. We passed her. She was on that sidewalk, and we were on this one.

"She's different. Seems like someone new," said Cok as he nudged me with his elbow. I agreed with a snort because I was also spellbound and my head was turning past my shoulder to look at her longer. Truly, she was a girl that people could not just take one glance at, much less out of the corner of the eye in passing. It was the same for both men and women. If you ask me, the main factors were her lascivious walk, which made her breasts even more provocative, and her curvaceous body. Her hair which was so wildly curly, her red lipstick and her arching eyebrows were each a point of attraction. Her dark red satin overcoat was the thing that first caught the eye when spotting her from afar.

I agreed with Cok's guess that this girl was new here or just passing through our town. However, I was hesitant because at that time girls who came from other cities or regions always wore dresses of the latest fashion, at that time known as the "New Look." Her long dress came down to her ankles and had loose sleeves. And she wasn't wearing a dress of the latest fashion. So I thought she certainly couldn't be from outside our region.

The second time I saw her, Cok saw her first because of his long legs. "That's her," he said nudging me. I was still angry from just being in a movie theater overflowing with spectators, and in my anger I suddenly realized that there was someone passing by who was drawing everyone's attention. My eyes like laser beams looked all over for "that's her." "A different kind of different," I said when I saw "that's her."

People jostled like ducks to get out of the way and step aside for her, gawking like they wanted to leave their buddies behind. Men and women did the same thing. And "that's her" acted like she was fully aware that she had become the center of attention. She passed, sticking out her chest which was already sticking out. Young kids out of passion tried to bump into "that's her" as though it were unintentional, or acted like a male turkey showing off for a female.

I don't know how it happened, but eventually we became friends with "that's her." I followed her like a shadow. I wanted to know what it was that made her so attractive that Cok always nudged me when he saw her and that made me haltingly comment "a different kind of different." Because as a sculptor I wanted to know what kind of girl had the ability to attract generally, the kind of girl who I would make my model "wooden girl." From her face, there was not a single thing that could be taken as a model. Her eyebrows and eyes were perfectly normal. Her nose, well, other girls had more of a sharp nose. Her flat lips covered her prominent teeth. Her jaw was a bit big. Her skin had never once been the object of praise by romantic authors.

Her name was Maria. When she wrote it out it always became Maria Yusran, with the addition being a combination of her father and mother's names. Her age was twenty-three years old. It's an age that's still young for adults. But she would pick an argument about that, saying "Aren't I a mature, adult woman?!" And her eyes would narrow, too, and her brows would furrow. At first I thought, this is a girl marked for obstinance. At the very least, from the way she talks it was clear that she liked to do whatever was forbidden and taboo for women to do, or she was not about to do anything that was seen as a woman's responsibility. But that didn't mean she didn't like sweeping the house and the yard or working in the kitchen.

"I want a clean room, a clean yard. What's wrong with me making it that way? Same thing with kitchen work. But don't look at it as work just for women," she would say when we got caught up in talking about differences in function between men and women in and outside the household.

"The difference between men and women is just biological. It's not in social functions," she said, digging in her heels to defend the position.

Once she had already made statements like that, what else could I say? It was useless to say that the social difference between men and women had arisen because of the biological difference. Even in our own Minangkabau homeland, where all people, male and female, are of the same status, all housework is the women's responsibility. Men lose face if they do housework.

"Just go ahead," she would always say if someone gave her the opportunity to go first through a door or any other form of social etiquette. "That kind of etiquette is medieval. It's an etiquette based on the view that women are weak creatures that must be helped. I don't like that," she said. It was the same way that time we were climbing Mount Merapi and she fell down; she didn't want to be helped. She got up by herself and started walking by herself despite a limp. "If a woman falls, oooh, all the men want to help her. Watch when a man falls, all of them act as if they don't care," she said.

"Yeah. It's really too much. But women are also too much; if a woman falls, or even a man, there are no women who want to help. 'It's the men's job,' they say," I teased.

She wouldn't put up with that kind of teasing. Normally she would hit you if she felt offended. Though, for the longest time she didn't want to hit me or pinch me if she was offended, because she knew I liked to be abused by women like that.

I am still amused to this day by how she would bounce back and forth because of her excitement in speaking, putting forward her point of view. She would sit upright and straight. Her head held high. The look in her eye was intense and her lips stiff. Nevertheless, if she laughed, it was like this world had never been lonely. It really felt good to hear the sound of her laugh.

There was one thing I could never get her to talk about, and that was her choices for her future. Her dreams. Her hopes. Her career. What kind of household she wanted. Her ideal husband and number of kids. It was almost as if the future and the past were not even important enough to be topics of discussion. It was as though, if today were Wednesday, then yesterday or tomorrow were also Wednesday.

ଔ

There was one time when I went over to her place and found her really depressed. When she sat facing me, she was silent. She sat with her chin in her hands and the look in her eyes was like it would pass straight through any object in front of her. Including me. It was as if I were not even there. If I asked her something her answers were scattered. But I knew that her acting like this was not her trying to chase me out. And I also knew that she wanted someone to talk to. So I waited.

She worked in an agency that originally had not had female employees. Because it wanted to be fashionable, the agency took in three girls. Rita, the niece of the Chief, became his secretary. Delly was for the Vice-Chief, while Maria herself was assigned to the general staff. Delly eventually became her close friend. They went to and from the office together. And in the end they moved into the same apartment. The experiences of those two were almost the same, working in an office that was short on work but long on workers.

Being an employee among dozens of men wasn't exactly a situation that made Maria happy. She said spending time with employees the same age as her was like spending time with clueless, superficial people. Spending time with the older ones, she just got strange stories. When she held herself aloof, all kinds of bad things were said about her. The more time passed the more she came to differ in how she spent time with the people in her office. But that was not what made her resentful, or what made her depressed.

Sometimes Maria would tell stories about incidents at her office until she would laugh heartily with amusement. There was a time when she was brought by her boss to a job out of town. Sometimes they used a driver and sometimes not. At first it was safe. Her boss acted like a polite and good-natured man. But, eventually he acted like one of those men. Grabbing here, grabbing there, every time they were in the sedan car. At first she was heartsick and offended. But what could she say, except to reject him politely? "It's tough, right, dealing with a man like that who's your boss," she said, explaining her experience as a female employee who has to obey her boss.

Later the attitude of her boss changed, becoming like "one of those men" as a regular routine, someone who took advantage of his underlings. The change made Maria chuckle as she told me about it. She said her boss wanted to go out of town. He brought her along. That time they came home late. Maria wasn't afraid, because they had a driver. "Whew, during the trip home, he hugged me and tried to kiss me. He thought I wouldn't scream because I would be ashamed to be found out by the driver. I actually didn't scream. But I scratched his mouth with my long nails. 'You feel this,' I said in my heart when he was hurt but wasn't brave enough to whimper. He was also ashamed to be found out by the driver. He let me go. The next day when we met in the office, he didn't change his attitude toward me. What surprised me were his words, 'If all female employees became cats like you, the whole office would be safe.' Now doesn't that have all kinds of meanings?" she declared.

Maria could not deny those incidents. She also could not deny that Delly's boss did the same thing. But Delly's method was more refined. She did not mess around with scratching. She could be free from her boss's temptation by threatening to report him to his wife. "It seems Delly's boss also has no guts," Maria said about Delly's experience.

Maria regretted the opinion commonly held by men about obedient female employees who could be tempted and wooed by their bosses. "Why does every boss have to show his manliness? Even though all of them just go on the government's payroll? Why don't men see female employees as social equals with men? If they both fall in love, that's normal. But when you want to molest or find an outlet for your lust, it's barbaric," Maria commented bitterly.

"So in the end, Delly's pregnant," she said after I had waited a long time to find out what had made her so depressed. "I was disappointed. Sad for the both of them. Delly always said there wasn't anything going on between her and Tajak, her boss. Turns out she's already six months pregnant. It's even more personal than that: I live in the same room with her. Every month she still uses a pad. I've been lied to for so long. But that's not it. If she likes that man, why not just marry him? Why do you have to get six months pregnant first, then say something? That man, if he likes Delly, why does he have to make such a scandal? Why does Delly have to suffer through six months first, then share the problem?"

I was really surprised, too, that Delly was already six months pregnant. However, I tried not to react.

"What makes me heartsick is Tajak's answer when I asked him why he didn't get married in the first place. Why did he have to wait six months? But what was his answer? 'I didn't have a reason to marry Delly. But after she was already pregnant, yeah, what else could I do?' When I asked him if Delly hadn't gotten pregnant? 'Yeah, no need to marry, right?' That was his answer. Meaning, Delly has been made a simple concubine. That's how awful he is."

"Why did Delly have to wait until six months?" I asked.

"At first they wanted to abort it. After that didn't work out, they started talking about marriage. And what if Delly died from the abortion, what then? I'm disgusted."

"If there's no response or request from the woman, will the man be able to do anything?" I said, without meaning to defend Tajak.

Maria got riled up. She was on fire again. She said, "Men always talk like that. It's all the women's fault. It's women who ruin the world. It's women who cause men to be corrupt, to cheat, to break their promises. All men say that women are as evil as gambling, drunkenness, opium, and stealing. All men, including you, say that men are instinctively polygamous. Because of that women become tempting. There's no man who remembers about the heart of a woman, like Delly, when they are seduced or molested by their own boss. Ugh, I'm sick of talking about it."

With the intent of tempering her dejection, I said that civilization was built by men. Because biologically, men were fated to be stronger. So all norms, even state regulations, were organized based on the point of view of men's needs. Although various laws have held up the equality of men and women, the administration of many regulations continued to put women in a place of being only part of a man, not his companion. That was civilization.

"Stop your preaching," she said scorchingly.

I knew who and what Maria was about; I did not respond to her attitude. I was even whistling. Later she swatted me with the chair cushion.

Eventually Maria also got married. She chose Cok as her husband after two years of knowing him. A few days before her wedding, Maria told me with a happy face, "You know what? When we began to get to know each other, I put down you and Cok on my list of nominated husband candidates. But you lost, because Cok is better able to control me. You remember that day we wanted to meet up before? The meeting room was so dirty. Cok gave me a broom and told me to sweep. Remember? Because of that I chose Cok."

Later I teased her by saying, "I didn't suspect that an emancipated woman still needed a man who could control her."

Once more I was swatted with the chair cushion.

ଔ

"When Cok was caught, he was scruffy. Like a real Fidel Castro. After he had been held one month, he was interrogated, he was beaten while in detention, he was carried to the bank of this river to be shot. Maria, who was with Cok when he was caught, didn't want to let go of him when was about to be shot. She kept hugging Cok. In times of war, people don't act and think right. When the Sten gun fired, both of them collapsed and fell into these swiftly flowing waters. Nobody even knows whether the bodies have been found," Johor told me, narrating the end of Maria's life.

I stood dazed for a long time, staring at the waters of the Antokan River flowing toward the Indian Ocean. But inside my head thoughts welled up; why in a civil war must people kill prisoners who have already surrendered?

A Hero's Tale

It was awfully hot inside the bus, even though the wind was whipping in through the windows. The road was horrible. Full of potholes. It was even worse if you were sitting in the back row, squeezed in between two sweating fat people, making it harder to breathe. That's where I was stuck. I tried to switch seats, but no luck. I leaned forward as best I could. I mean, my back was no longer up against the seat, so I felt like I had a little bit of space. I began to feel relieved. And I got a bit more space when I stretched my feet out under the row facing me. Actually, the only things that stretched out were my calves—my pant legs didn't follow. And my bare calves brushed briefly against the calves of the cute girl sitting in front of me, facing the back of the bus, right in my line of vision. So, I can say that it happened pretty often that our eyes met. And at the moments when my calf brushed her calf I felt embarrassed, as if my character was becoming rather compromised. I wanted to pull myself back up, but I couldn't manage. I was feeling kind of sore, which hampered my willingness to move. If there hadn't been a reaction from the calves of that cute girl, I would have calmed my heart by thinking about any old thing. I coaxed my heart to ignore the moral peril by praising myself, thinking "I'm a good guy."

The girl whose face was displayed in front of me was really fantastically cute. Her face was the kind that would lead to romantic daydreams in the mind of any man, even a cleric. She was a village girl from an Islamic school. She had pink silk covering her head and a traditional dress of *batik* cloth. If I didn't misunderstand the shouts of my heart, there was an unusual tendency starting to emerge in me. I mean, my heart started to be a bit unfaithful to my wife. However, I didn't forbid my heart from leaping as much as it wanted to. I let it daydream as much as it liked. And I didn't feel like I was sinning at all with this laissez-faire attitude toward my heart.

I then affirmed a new life philosophy: that sin and betrayal are only punished if the heart advances a motion, and the brain agrees to it, and the other parts of the body follow it through in the way they want to. But if it's just the heart that advances a motion, while the brain abstains and the rest are totally silent, then my wife could rest easy with our existing treaty.

My heart was also praying (well, well; praying?), hoping that the conditions and situation we were in would not change until the bus reached my town. And that meant I could continue to let my heart leap, advance a motion, put forward resolutions, and propose initiatives for another two-and-a-half hours. And occasionally I would get giddy remembering the actions of my heart, which was behaving like a member of parliament pretentiously engaging in the trappings of democracy. I felt how this world is really safe and comfortable. I forgot about the atmosphere of the bus with its awful bouncing. My nose didn't sense the provocative stench of the sweat from the people on either side of me.

My heart returned like a teenager to daydreaming on and on and on. Then all of a sudden a driving rain poured down on us relentlessly. All the windows of the bus were closed up in a hurry, so the heat of the air was that much more oppressive. Despite this, my heart kept daydreaming without a care in the world.

Just as suddenly as the rain had come, the bus stopped with a jolt. And all of these sudden happenings caused my heart to shake suddenly, too. It turns out the cute girl wanted to get off. And all of a sudden I felt like a dog who had lost its bone. When that girl

wanted to stand up and take her calves out of there, her hand—
which was covered in diamonds—leaned on my knee. Seeing the
sparkle of that expensive stuff made my heart, which had advanced
so many motions, shrivel up. I felt how little my self-worth actually
was. And when my mind laughed at my shriveling heart, my heart
shouted out in anger, "Watch out if I win the lottery!"

But all of a sudden, too, another person grabbed my attention.
The man who was sitting to the left of the cute girl also followed
her to get off the bus. Questions rose up in the depths of my heart,
"Who is he? Is he her husband? Her fiancé? What's up with this
guy?" And on the flip side of my curiosity, there emerged a sense
of jealousy and doubt. All of this kept building up and began to
take over all the other feelings inside me. As though the whole
world was bad in every way, and only I was a good guy. Even if
this were not the case, if I were to be a painter looking for human
models, surely I would take that man as a model of the worst of
humankind.

The doubt flaring up in my heart forced me to get off the bus,
too. I had forgotten that if you want to take an action, your good
sense has to weigh in first. I forgot all about my habit of being
patient and staying calm. I became a man who wanted to follow
the words of his heart, my heart that was suspicious. And there
was good reason for my suspicion. I didn't get off that bus into the
torrential rain on that empty street for nothing.

I saw the cute girl had turned right, onto a little street that had
become swampy, inundated with water. That bastard, that awful
man also turned. A fair distance behind the girl. From the eyes of
the bastard, deep pits like the eyes of Dracula in a movie, I saw shine
the fires of hell reaching toward the cute girl. My heart jumped.
One of three things was bound to happen. One, the bastard would
steal her gold and diamonds. Two, he would steal the girl's dignity.
Three, he would steal both of them in one go.

The narrow little street, turning this way and that, got further and further from the main road. Of course, that would make it easy for the terrible bastard to let fly his lust. And as the story goes, in the olden times of the mythical figure Cindur Mato, this area was entirely uninhabited. Plenty of folks had already lost life and limb and all their possessions there. Just thinking about it, I already felt how harrowing it was—this incident that was about to happen. But because of this, it made me feel like I would become a hero. A hero for this cute girl whose calves had pressed against my calves. I didn't care if I had to put my life on the line. I carefully followed them. Like a cat hunting its prey. No. Not like a cat, but like a tiger. I had to be careful so they wouldn't know that I was the one and only hero that would defend the honor of this girl who was under threat. And I waited for the critical moment. When I then appeared heroically to defend this cute girl, surely the bastard would be shocked and ask for mercy. Meanwhile the girl, filled with joy and gratitude, would throw herself into my arms. Just like the movies I always watched.

I was certain I would get those calves again. So clean and fair-skinned, even more than I had thought at first. I didn't feel the pouring rain anymore. My body didn't feel cold and soaked in the downpour; it felt warm. I really, truly felt myself to be the strongest man on earth. One who could, with just one strike, break the neck of this bastard into three pieces.

Then the terrible bastard walked faster, and from his waistband he pulled out a gun. And he shouted savagely telling the girl to stop. The girl, who didn't realize anyone was following her, was startled and ran this way and that. But the bastard was faster. The girl was frightened, and she fell forward. And the huge body of the bastard was suddenly on top of her. The girl struggled and cried out for help at the top of her lungs. But none of it made any difference. The pouring rain put a damper on her cries. I couldn't take it anymore. I pulled out my gun, too. I wanted to go wild, I wanted to risk my life, I wanted to free the girl from having her person and her heart crushed, I wanted to show what kind of man I was. I wanted to kill the wicked bastard and drink his blood to my heart's satisfaction. Who else would defend the honor of this cute girl under threat if it wasn't me? Who else?

But ... there wasn't actually a gun in my waistband. Actually, I had never had one. I always shrank away at even the sight of a gun. I became crestfallen. And as that new feeling arrived, my heroism flew away. Every bit of it flew off and left me there, until I was like a sinful beggar who saw the good looks, greatness, and power of other people as their proper right. I felt I was the size of a bristle that had fallen off its broom. I looked at my fists—they couldn't even kill a rat. And the cavity of my chest—if the bastard's fist punched me even once, it wouldn't be more than a week before people carried me from the hospital to the grave.

And my wife would have to carry the full responsibility for seven children. My good sense came back to me. And I couldn't bring myself to let my wife carry all that responsibility, lose her happiness, lose her hope, disappointed and worrying all her life because of my death. If my death was the proper kind of death, not the death of a beaten dog, no one would blame me if my corpse were laid flat. But wouldn't my wife feel beaten down because her husband died trying to defend someone else, Lord knows who? How would her heart feel if I died because I was defending a girl who was to become my mistress? Her heart would be all the more hurt, and it would sting her to the core.

Slowly the old warning of my grandmother came back to me: "If you want to be safe, avoid fighting." But now I was searching for a fight. And I would die because of that fight? I felt I was rebelling against my grandmother's wisdom. If the bastard did something wicked, well, it was because he was a terrible bastard. On the other hand, I was a good guy. And hadn't my religion teacher once taught me, "Your works will fall on your head, others' works will fall on their heads"? Sins and merits were like that too, I figured. And I suddenly became so very loyal to all the things I had once been taught about staying safe. And I returned to my reputable character, as a man who was patient and surrendered to God. If all of humankind had a reputable character like me, I was sure the world would be saved.

So I didn't want to see what was happening, because I didn't want to have that sin on my shoulders. I snuck behind the trunk of a durian tree. I hid myself. So the bastard would not know that I knew about his wicked actions. And bastards get incredibly mad if other people find out what bastards they really are.

Slinking away, I returned to the main road. And when I reached the side of the main road and a bus stopped, I climbed aboard as fast as lightning. Just my luck, when I got on board the bus my shoulder was struck by the damn bastard, who had apparently gotten on before me. I was startled and flailed about with a fierceness that I didn't think I had in me. But everyone around me laughed—laughing at me, actually. I looked them in the eye one by one, until they shrank back.

But I just embarrassed myself, because I came to realize that my head had slumped forward, and I had actually been dreaming. And when my head had slumped forward, the man who looked like a bastard had apparently held onto my shoulder in a friendly way. When I began to pull myself together, it turned out that from when the cute girl got off, I had fallen asleep and started dreaming. Dreaming more and more fantastical betrayals of my wife.

However, I began to get anxious with myself because I was aware that I really come from a nation of cowards. Maybe it's true what the experts say: that dreams are a kind of reflection of a person's true self.

Pride and Joy

Everybody, old and young, big and small, called him Ompi. He would be a bit embarrassed if he were called anything else. And no one wanted to embarrass the old man.

In his youth, Ompi had been a clerk in the Dutch Resident's office. So he had been able to put together a pretty decent amount of wealth. Ever since his wife passed away twelve years ago, all his attention was poured into their only child, a son. At first the child was named Edward. But because of the English king who abdicated the throne over a woman, the name Edward was switched for Ismail, like the name of the first king of Egypt. When the news circulated that a man named Ismail was punished for being a thief and a murderer, Ompi became enraged. It was as though his child's name was also being besmirched. And he felt insulted. And on a day chosen according to the beliefs of the elders, when the moon was waxing, Ompi held a ritual feast. Thus, Ismail became Indra Budiman. However, the kid still clung to the name that he had chosen for himself: Eddy.

Ompi became annoyed. But because he loved his child, he also accepted that name, so long as Indra Budiman was tagged onto the back of it. So his name was officially set as Eddy Indra Budiman. It didn't change after that. However, in Ompi's heart, he still dreamt of another addition to the front end of his son's current name. There were plenty of candidates for what could be added. And one of them would have to be added, even if it meant exhausting all of his wealth. But this was not the kind of addition that could be accomplished with just a ritual feast. It was the times and the situation that would determine it. Ompi was sure the time would come. And he restrained himself through all that waiting. One glorious day in the future, this dream would surely turn into a reality. He was sure that his Indra Budiman would get the addition "Doctor" in front of his current name. Or another equally dignified title. When Ompi began to dream about that addition to the name, he picked up pencil and paper. He wrote down his child's name, "Dr. Indra Budiman." And Ompi felt so very happy. He assured his neighbors that this goal would definitely be reached.

If someone passed away after a long illness, he would say, "Oh, I double my condolences, because I couldn't manage to avoid this calamity. See now, if my child, Indra Budiman, were already a doctor, this death could have definitely been prevented."

And if Ompi saw someone building a house, he would say, "Oh, bless your heart. Our people's houses are still old-fashioned in their architecture. See now, if my child, Indra Budiman, were already an engineer, surely he could help people to make houses that were more beautiful."

From the time when Indra Budiman left for Jakarta, Ompi was even more sure, year after year, that all of his goals would definitely be reached. And it was true. As it turned out, every semester Indra Budiman would send a school report with fantastic grades. And every year he graduated on to the next class. In just two years, Indra Budiman finished his high school degree with a diploma and a high grade point average.

When Ompi read the letter from his son telling him about this accomplishment, his eyes glistened with tears of joy. "Oh, my child," he said to himself, "I'm so proud. It is good that you become a doctor. Because so many people need this. In that way people will look up to you. And as for money—what is three thousand, five thousand for me to send? Go on and buy clothes that are fitting for a medical student. Spending money of three hundred and fifty a month? Of course I'll send it, my child. Why not?"

And from that time on, Ompi was a bit impatient about the slow passing of time, like an engaged man waiting for the day of his wedding. But everybody knew, it wasn't even a secret anymore, that Ompi's goals would only remain a dream. However, how could folks tell him, if the old man didn't want to believe it? Even worse, he would berate and accuse people of being jealous of the progress his son had achieved. And he would immediately send even more money, without thinking of the consequences. And that was merely to challenge the gossip that sullied his son's good name.

"These days people with dirty mouths are gossiping about you, my child. But your father understands, they want to slander you just because they are jealous of your dignified life. Become a doctor quick as you can, so we can plug their wicked mouths," he wrote in one of his letters.

And eventually people began to feel sorry for Ompi. No one would badmouth Indra Budiman to him anymore. The opposite, in fact—it was as though everyone had made a pact to praise him.

"Wow, Ompi's boy. He's the real thing. If he's not off to school, he's sure to be memorizing his lessons at home," said one fellow who had just come back from Jakarta, answering a question from Ompi.

"Off to school? Why would he go off to school?" Ompi felt offended. "A medical student doesn't memorize, don't you know? He *studies*. He doesn't go 'off to school.' He goes to campus."

"Oh, yes, yes of course Ompi. That's what I meant."

"I had already figured that my son, Indra Budiman, was a good kid. He's sure to be a success. I'm so proud. Aw, you should come over to my house today for lunch. I'll slaughter a chicken."

Other folks who had migrated away to make their fortunes and then returned said the same thing to Ompi. "Who doesn't know him? Indra Budiman. All of Jakarta knows who he is. All the girls are hoping for his affections."

Then Ompi shook his head with a smile. "The real thing. The real thing. That's Indra Budiman, my son. He really is a handsome boy. What kind of woman wouldn't be crazy about him? Ha ha ha. Oh, come round to my house later. I've got a treat for you."

Later, if Ompi met a pretty girl whom he knew, he would greet her saying: "Hey, you know my son, the medical student? Soon when he comes home, I'll introduce him to you. So he can propose to you. Ha ha ha."

The girl would always turn red in the face, because she felt offended. But according to Ompi, her red face was a sign of being embarrassed and bashful. And he would become even more pleased.

However, when Ompi found out I was to be married, he got a new inspiration. He felt that Indra Budiman was also already of the age to be set up. And in his reckoning, naturally his Indra Budiman would be pleased and become even more diligent in his quest for knowledge, to pay back his father who had never failed to look after all the needs of his son. And he kept hoping for people to come round and propose to his Indra Budiman. Because in our village, it was usually the woman's side that went out to make the proposal on her behalf. Of course it was clear that Ompi's hopes would never amount to more than hopes. But Ompi didn't want to understand. His kind of arrogance was easily offended. And his anger towards parents who had pretty girls for daughters was no small thing. It was actually quite a big thing when Ompi blew up at someone, if he knew that they were marrying off their pretty daughters without thinking of Indra Budiman first. It made no sense, how people didn't seek after his son, the soon-to-be doctor. After a while, his feeling of vengeance towards them was like a burning heat. "Better watch out soon. Once my Indra Budiman is a doctor, I'll spit in all your faces, you haughty fools."

He never said anything about his anger to Indra Budiman. The opposite, in fact. He told him that many people with pretty girls came round to propose to him. But he had rejected all of them. Because he firmly believed that his Indra Budiman prioritized his studies over women. And besides that, a medical student wouldn't want to be with a village girl who was backwards to boot. "Go ahead and choose a girl in Jakarta, my son. A girl who is fitting for your future station," he said to close his letter.

The bad news was this changed the thinking of Indra Budiman, who all this time had thought that he wouldn't be wanted by the folks of his village. Now, he really believed that lots of folks had come courting. It didn't occur to him that his lies to his father all this time were already known to the people of his village. He forgot that his wanton lifestyle did not escape the eyes of all the people from his village who lived in Jakarta. From that time on, the actor and the audience switched places. If before it had been the child who was lying and the father who believed it, now it was the father who was pulling a trick, and the child who was believing it. Then the son expressed his wish to his father that he send some of the photos of girls who had been put forward.

To prove the truth of his letters, Ompi sent any pictures of girls that he happened to have. He didn't care if the photo was of a girl who was married or engaged. He didn't even care if the girl had already died. He kept sending them, with hopes that his son wouldn't like any of them. And how pleased Ompi was when not a single one of the photos he sent drew the attention of his son's heart. Besides that, he knew, too, that the fakery of this play would end at some time in the future. His son would surely eventually know, and with that there would arise another difficulty that wouldn't be easy to resolve.

But as it turns out, God had pity on this father who loved his son. At just the moment when Ompi had run out of pictures of girls, all of a sudden the letters from Indra Budiman stopped arriving. Stuck between troubled and relieved, Ompi was preoccupied waiting for a letter from his son. Like a hungry tiger in a cage waiting for someone to give him meat. Sick of waiting, he sent a letter. He waited a few days. But no response came. He sent another. He waited. There was no reply to this one either. He sent. He waited. He never got a reply. Months came and went. Ompi was left waiting and waiting.

One fateful day, when Ompi had begun to lose hope, the postman arrived with a fistful of letters in his hand. So Ompi's heart began to race. He was trembling with joy. But how that old man's heart was crushed, because it turned out that the mail carrier was just delivering letters that had been returned. He couldn't believe that the letters were returned. He felt like he was dreaming and his body was as light as cotton blown around by the wind. He turned the letters over and over in his hands. Then he opened them and read them one by one. And he knew that all of them were the letters that he had sent to his son. But he couldn't really believe it. He even tried to convince himself that he was dreaming. And he prayed to God that what was happening was really a dream.

From then on, everything became terrible. He fell ill, even to the point of delirium. And because his appetite was gone, Ompi suffered even more. Body and soul. Now in his life there was just one thing he was looking for. That was, a letter. A letter from his son, his Indra Budiman. It was as though his whole life began to dim like a candle whose wick is burnt up. And he laid on his cot, unwilling to move. But his eyes were always wide open looking at the top of the mosquito net. His eyes looked bigger every day as his body got skinnier and skinnier. But his wide eyes had no brightness to them. They were dim.

However, every afternoon, between four and five o'clock, Ompi looked like a sick man about to get well. And he was strong enough to stand up and go to the front door. And the light in his eyes began to shine again. Because at that time the postman would usually come to deliver letters to their destinations. But moments like that, which gave him a time of happiness and hope, were also the times that cut him even deeper, so the sickness got worse. Because the postman never came by again bringing a letter from Indra Budiman. And if the postman passed by without stopping, Ompi's eyes dimmed again.

But the bad luck kept piling up. What happened was Ompi fell on his tailbone. It was a long time before anyone realized and came to carry him to his cot in the bedroom. Ompi became paralyzed, and that was the end of Ompi waiting by the front door each afternoon. Now he waited stretched out on his cot. He asked for a mirror to be hung on the wall to give a view of the front door, so he would be able to see the postman bring a letter from Indra Budiman right when it happened. And from that time on, every day from four until five o'clock, his eyes were glued on that mirror. Just at that time. Meanwhile, at other times it was like Ompi didn't care about anything.

After the third time, we never called the doctor again, because doctor's visits only served to deepen the wounds in his heart. The presence of the doctor made his heart restless because he remembered Indra Budiman, who was due to become a doctor but who never sent letters anymore. The doctor's visits were seen as needling, that his son still hadn't been able to make his dreams into a reality.

The last time that I met with the doctor, who already didn't want to come anymore, he just shook his head. "I can't treat him anymore. Look for another doctor. Or take him to the hospital.

If none of that is possible, don't leave him alone. If needed, even though the risk is great, indulge his flights of fancy again."

From that time on, in rotation with other people, I made myself available to always be nearby Ompi. I knew full well that there was no hope of making him live any longer. That was the reason I didn't tell him that my wedding day was already upon us. Because I was afraid that news would just make his suffering even worse. Besides that I built up his precious hopes in a vague way that Indra Budiman might come back. I made up stories of memories of old times and aspirations for the future that made him happy. I told these stories with a sheepish heart.

Even I knew none of it was any use. There was just one thing he wanted. A letter from Indra Budiman. A letter saying that he had graduated and got the title of "Doctor." Sometimes I had an urge to write the letter myself. But I was always up in the air, even afraid, in case that move might have consequences that were even more grave. So I never tried to write it.

One day the thing that I had suspected would happen happened. This was the thing I had been dreading. I saw the postman go into the yard of Ompi's house. That was around eleven o'clock in the morning. I knew he couldn't possibly be carrying a letter. It had to be a telegram. And tucked away in that telegram there was sure to be something critical. In a hurry I went to head off the postman at the front door. My intention was to open the telegram and know what was inside it before anything else. And if needed I would change what was inside, so as to avoid the horrifying something it held.

But everything happened so very quickly and my plans failed. I didn't have time to open the letter. Because, without me suspecting it at all, Ompi who had been paralyzed all this time, was suddenly standing right behind me. Right at the moment I was receiving and signing for the telegram. Ompi's shaking legs were holding up his wrinkled body. His hand was holding the back of a chair. And I lost all faith in my own eyes. What strength could cause Ompi to be able to stand and even to walk? I didn't know.

"Open it. Read what's inside right away," Ompi said like he was ordering folks around back in his younger days.

I ripped open the light-yellow packet with a trembling hand. In an instant I knew that the critical moment had come. The telegram announced that Indra Budiman had passed away.

"A telegram from my son? What does he say? Is he coming home with his new title of 'Doctor?'" Ompi asked with a voice that wheezed but was in a hurry to escape his throat.

I didn't know what I should say. And I hoped for a miracle of the Lord to free me from that torture. But the miracle didn't come. I nodded. While in my heart I screamed, the thing that was going to happen had happened.

Ompi sat down in the chair. His eyes were bright. His hands stretched out to me asking for the telegram. I was afraid to give it to him. But I couldn't do anything else. I put the telegram into his hands. He gripped the telegram tightly. Then he squeezed it tightly to his chest. "Finally it came, the thing I've been waiting for," he said.

The silence was so oppressive that I could hear the beating of my own heart.

"Oh, no. I won't read this telegram. I am afraid the joy would make my heart explode. You read it out for me. Read it out slowly. So that word by word it can spread through all my nerve endings," said Ompi, haltingly.

In a panic I put together something that risked my soul and almost became a regret for the rest of my life. I would make up a tale to make his heart glad. But the telegram was not given to me.

It was still held on his chest in an embrace. And at the same time his lips curved into a smile, and his eyes shone bright with light.

"No need to read it out. I'm not strong enough to listen to it. I'll suffocate from the happiness that came wrapped up in here. I want to get healthy. I want to be strong first. So that this explosion of joy won't kill me. Call a doctor. Go on, call him. So I can be all fresh when my son, Doctor Indra Budiman, comes. Go on. Call the doctor," Ompi said with joy.

And he raised the telegram to his lips. He kissed it with affection. He kissed it for a long time while his eyes remained closed. A long time, until his hands dropped, and his eyes opened again after they had lost their light. And the telegram fell and floated to his lap.

Comings and Goings

When Masri's first letter arrived, the man's longing to meet him the following year soared. He kissed the letter over and over, and tucked it away between the pages of the Quran. Every day he read the Quran, and each time he kissed the letter. And all those sentences he cherished always drew his eye. Even though the sentences were stuck fast in his memory, he still read them again.

"Please come, Father. There is a burning desire in our hearts to see you. Don't you want to meet Arni, your daughter-in-law? And your two grandchildren, Masra and Irma?"

"Yes, of course, my son. Of course. Why not? I'm getting on. Before I die I must meet up with you all," said the old man in his heart. Then he felt around on the right side of his chest, trying to find something in the inside pocket of his jacket. And then his hand disappeared behind the folds of his jacket. Just for a moment. It came out with an envelope with worn edges. He opened the envelope and brought out a photo the size of postcard. He stared with round eyes, and his lips curved inward, etching a smile of satisfaction.

"You have a moustache now, Masri. You've really changed. So you're happy with Arni? You already have two children. I'm happy for you, my child. I've always felt happy seeing a happy household. Especially yours, my child." Then he put the postcard back in the envelope. When it was only half way back in he took it out again and brought it to his lips. It didn't reach them—he remembered

there were people around him. And he put the postcard back in the
envelope. He put it away again in his jacket pocket. He leaned back
in a leisurely fashion and his memories drifted to a bygone time.

When Masri was three years old, the man's beloved wife had
died. At the time the man was still young, and his heart was broken.
He felt as if he would never feel happiness again. The loneliness
constantly assailed him. It was so quiet. It was unbearable. And
when it came in the night when he couldn't sleep a wink, it was
nerve-shredding. So eventually he remarried.

But in fact, the marriage just hurt him further. His heart, still
dwelling on the love of Masri's departed mother, was rent asunder
by the coming of this woman. He didn't want anything to change.
The way the house was kept, the way the food was prepared, he
wanted them just as they'd been done by Masri's mother. But his
new wife was not going to let her husband wallow in the past. And
they were not happy. They often fought, and eventually divorced,
despite his wife being pregnant at the time.

After a long time, he married again. But he eventually divorced
again. Then he married and divorced again. And he felt that family
life could never give him happiness again. So, the loneliness in his
heart was filled by women who wouldn't bind him with the duties
of marriage.

"Ah, Masri's mother was one of a kind. There was only one
woman like her. She was kind. Very kind. Everyone liked her.
Everyone. And she was talented. She was good at everything. But,
you know, God is too quick in taking everything a person loves. Ah,
I don't understand why all good-hearted people leave the people
who love them too soon. I don't understand why it has to be that
way. Or is it that the world can only be inhabited by people who
are not good? Ah, so this world cannot become heaven on earth?"
he muttered in his ruminations. He shook his head, his eyes welling
up in a crescendo of sorrow. He took off his glasses, then massaged

the skin under his eyes, stopping his tears from falling. He put his glasses back on. He leaned back again in his seat.

His train raced along. The people around him had already drifted off into a doze. Their heads nodded like swaying dolls' heads. Indeed, some of them were sound asleep, saliva dribbling from the corner of their lips like snot dribbling from a runny nose. There were some whose heads nodded, then when it seemed their head would fall into their lap, they woke again. But the old man still had his eyes wide open. He cast his gaze out the window. Outside was a verdant backdrop, covered by clouds fading to white in the sky. In the distance birds of prey flew intently. Then everything faded, dimmed by his memories of Masri, his son.

He was cast adrift for a long time, filling the emptiness with a desire for the company of women through the night. It destroyed his life. To the point that Masri, who was nurtured with his love, was tormented by his friends teasing him at school. However, his child still did not believe that his father's virtue had been corrupted. His child wanted evidence. His child wanted to see with his own eyes: was what his friends said about his father true? And his child snooped on him, and glimpsed his father in the embrace of that prostitute. How it broke the child's heart. Perhaps he wanted to blind himself, so that he could not see what was in front of his eyes. He approached his father with an uncontrollable hatred. Masri turning up was a source of mockery for the woman he'd paid, and he felt insulted and very angry. But it was his child that became the target of his anger. He slapped him as hard as he could. However, the child, in his pain, did and said nothing. His father could do what he liked.

"You insolent little... you make me ashamed. Go on, leave. You're no longer my child!"

"Certainly, I'm not the child of a father like this. I want to leave!" the boy protested.

"You're an insolent little…"

"If I'm insolent, it's not my fault. It's your actions that made me this way. It was you who caused me to be born without my agreement! After I was born, it was you who messed things up again!"

The father now had really lost his patience. If earlier the prostitute he'd paid had laughed at him, now it was his own child who was insulting him. He went to hit him again, but the child took off, never to return to his father's house.

The father felt like he couldn't breathe. His heartbeat pounded rapidly. He became aware again, breaking free of his daydream. He contemplated, consciously thinking clearly. "Things really went too far," he said in his heart. "What Masri said really hurt me. Of course, he wouldn't have spoken like that if I wasn't his father. Surely other people's children wouldn't say that to their father. Of course, it's me the father at fault—I'm a bad father. If I think about it now, Masri, I'd feel laid bare if I met you again. I'm truly not a good father. But, my child, what you said before was true. Your words brought me back to my senses. Late at night when I lay in bed in our home, gradually I became conscious of it. I was the one at fault. I'm a wretched father. But you'd already left, my child. Your going and not coming back broke my heart. I want you to always be by my side, because you're my only child. Because you're my world, the point I still cling onto. But you're no longer here. I want your forgiveness, child. I really want that moment to come. But you've never come.

"Then I repented, my child. I cast aside the worldly life. I sold all our possessions, and donated the proceeds. And I went to a distant village. I stayed in the mosque there. I surrendered myself to Allah. It lasted for years. And besides that, I tried to get those around me to live in harmony and peace. All of them, all the households in that village, joined me in bringing peace and happiness if there was discord. How happy I was in my heart, child, when I saw the happiness of their homes. Because I myself understood the meaning of a happy home.

"But, Masri, when I received your letter a year ago, I confess I hesitated at first to accept your invitation. I felt exposed. The child that I slapped, the child that I'd driven away, that child that was now inviting me to his house. I was ashamed. So ashamed, Masri. And I didn't want to come. Reluctant because of my shame. But do you know that I always kiss your letter?

"And then another letter came from you. Again, I didn't answer. And your third letter, along with a postal order, did not shake my heart from my initial hesitance. But, Masri, eventually I took the postal order to the post office. I was forced to, because there was someone else who I wanted to help with the money you'd sent. Since I'd taken your money, my child, I was forced to visit you as well. 'Forced' not meaning that I didn't want to, but because I was very ashamed to meet you.

"But at the same time, it comes to mind that I'm getting on. I don't have long left. And when I die, I don't want even the smallest bit of sin on me. My biggest sin will be erased by your forgiveness, my child. Now I am coming to surrender myself to you, as a failed father. You know, my child, that the letters that you sent tirelessly, four times without me answering, have broken down my bad traits—my pride, in being ashamed to ask forgiveness from someone younger. I realize now it's my arrogance that has wrecked my life for all this time."

"Are you OK, Mister? Why are you crying?" A voice entered the ears of the old man. He was startled from his ruminations. And he felt the tears above the corner of his mouth. He quickly wiped them away. Then he tried to smile sweetly at the inquirer. Then he directed his eyes out the window. He saw the blue-green nature split by houses in haphazard clumps. As time went on things got more crowded. But the train still raced on its way. He could hear the hisses of the locomotive chasing after one another. And they had almost reached the city.

As the train slowed down, his heart pounded all the harder. He was sure he would meet his child. And surely his child would give his heartfelt forgiveness. Surely. He felt how peaceful the world was. And when he died, he would die without carrying the burden of sin. In that peace, the train stopped. And in that veil of peace he went up the steps of his child's house. He didn't feel the slightest bit tired after the shaking of the train over almost a whole day. But his breathing tightened with the pounding of his heart, which thumped harder and harder, thumping like it had the first day he entered his wife's room. But he felt fresh. And he gulped in the air around his child's house as deeply as he could, so he could feel more at one with the beautiful life surrounding him. Facing to the west, to the north, to the east, and to the south. All the while on the line of his lips was etched a happy smile.

When he turned his body to face the door again, how surprised the old man was. The peace of nature that embraced him a moment ago was in a moment cast off, smashed to pieces. A woman, thin almost like a corpse, stood upright in the doorway with her arms on her hips, regarding him steadfastly. The old man, on the other hand, trembled, mesmerized by fear. He didn't understand why the woman had to be there. His thoughts were going so slowly. So he invited peaceful nature back with wholly good thoughts about the presence of the woman there.

"Why have you come, anyway?" asked the woman sharply. And the sharpness of the question grated as it entered the man's ears. He was offended. The arrogance that had settled for so long in the depths of his heart flared up red hot again. And with a gaze that burned with anger he said, "I came to my child's house. Because I was asked to come." But the words disappeared on his trembling lips. The sounds did not reach their target.

"If you have come to bring mischief, you can leave right now." The woman stiffened further.

"This house is my child's house. I came because I was called," the old man said again angrily.

But the woman did not hear anything from the mouth of the man standing upright like a statue in the doorway. And the woman spoke again. "But if you come with good intentions, come in."

And the old man did not want to argue on the stoop of his child's house. He entered with a hesitant heart full of questions. But the hesitancy was jettisoned when he looked around at the rooms in the house. It was very simple, but everything was neat and tidy. Clean. And what was most important was how harmonious it was. So, he knew that his child, Masri, lived in peace and happiness with his wife. He even began to feel happy. And he forgot for a moment the woman who was looking at him with wide eyes and a fearful heart.

"What happiness Masri has," he said as if to himself. "Surely Arni is a good match for him."

"All women are good matches for a man who knows how to value other people," said the woman bitingly.

And the man came up against the woman's presence again. He knew the woman's words were meant as a reproach to him. It was also a blow to remind him of his past life. He was offended. But he couldn't awaken the arrogance that had flared up earlier. Now he was left weak and unsteady by the blow. He reached for a chair. In his unsteadiness, he went over and over his distant past—all of the dark and bitter parts he remembered most clearly.

"Forgive me, Iyah. I really am not a good person. Being as old as this, not far from death even, I want things to be at peace and in good order. My wish is that when I die, I will die clean of the sins I committed," he said after a long time, with a hoarse voice and trembling words.

"Of course, an apology is easiest to say for someone who has known what it means to be happy in life," said the woman without losing her sharp tone. "But for me, someone who has always had difficulties, an apology has to be reckoned with first. A reckoning between you and me."

"Iyah," said the man again with a pleading tone, "For a long time, since I divorced you back then, I have regretted it." But not a word came out of his mouth except the woman's name.

"Now you've come just to cause trouble."

"Did you know I'd come?"

"I knew. But I always tried to make it so you wouldn't come. But I couldn't prevent you coming."

"Why did you want to prevent me?"

"Your coming would mess things up."

"But I've atoned. For a long time I've devoted my life to goodness. For a long time now I've understood why and how people should live."

"But you coming here has still brought sin."

"Brought sin? Why did I bring sin? Wasn't I asked to come here to…," he stopped a second, but then continued again. "What I mean is that I've come to ask forgiveness from my child. For the sake of the happiness of my child and his wife."

"Masri's wife is my child. Your child as well," said the woman sharply.

"Iyah," yelped the man with a hoarse voice. And suddenly his body was trembling, then he wilted, slumped on the support of the chair. He couldn't say another word. His thoughts and feelings seemed like shadows, jumbled, uneven, formless, filling the whole room. This went on for a long time. And when he became aware of himself again, he wasn't brave enough to open his eyes and see the reality around him. He wanted to try and think and consider all that had happened and that he'd experienced.

"Isn't it bitter for you to accept this reality? It was for me, too. When I knew they were siblings, from then until now I've readied myself to be damned. I'm willing to suffer all these sins, as long as they are still happy." Iyah's voice penetrated the ears of the man leaning back dazed in the chair.

"Why didn't you say anything?"

"Why would I say anything?"

And the man opened his eyes and asked again, "Isn't it a sin?"

"Truly it is. For those who know about it."

"Because of that, you let them go on not knowing?" He began to rouse himself again. "Whatever the case, they have to know. They have to. They must. It's essential."

Then his whole body became weak again. A moment later, with a hoarse, hissing voice, he continued with his words, "This is all a sin, Iyah. A great sin. A sin for us. A sin for me, a sin for you. A sin for them as well."

Not a single sound could be heard. All was still and silent. The thin woman with papery skin still stood stiffly in the same spot. All the while the man was still slumped against the chair's backrest.

"I have to tell them. After that they have to divorce. It has to be done. If all this time I've had God's blessing, why do I have to sully it toward the end of my life? So I must say something to them," said the old man, keeping his eyes closed, as if unwilling to see the reality.

He heard Iyah speak again. But her tone was derisive. "Oh, how selfish you are. You just want this so you can be free of the consequences of your past mistakes. To the point that now you want to destroy the happiness of your own children. Just because you are afraid to bear the punishment for your own sins."

"Iyah," he said weakly.

"Let them be happy in their ignorance," she insisted.

"I can't let that happen."

"Can't let that happen?"

"I'm not prepared to face God's damnation."

"Oh, so now you've learned how to say that. Why not before?"

He was hurt again. Wounded by Iyah's derision. Yet he knew that he was in the wrong. So he stayed quiet. But then when his duties and devotion to God came into his mind, he said with a firm voice and a level tone, "Iyah, whatever you say and however true the truth of what you say, there is another truth that we must uphold. God's truth. People have to be prepared to sacrifice themselves to uphold His commandments."

"Oh, so now you've learned how to talk about God's truth. Why? Just because you want to hide your own mistakes. Because you want to avoid the consequences of the things you did wrong in the past. Do you really think that you can seek forgiveness by surrendering yourself just like that without being brave enough to bear the risk of the mistakes you yourself have made?"

"Even so, I must tell them that they are siblings."

"To uphold the commandments of God?"

"To uphold the commandments of God, whom I worship day and night."

"Even though it will destroy other people's happiness."

"That's not the point—since people have reason, and must have faith."

"Bullshit. Your reason, your faith, it's just something to say to escape the fear of the reckoning for your mistakes."

"You're an apostate, Iyah!"

"Rather that than someone as cowardly as you!"

And the man felt that he didn't need to argue any more. He had already taken his decision. A decision that was in line with the beliefs he had upheld for years.

Iyah also felt that her opponent was unwilling to retreat from his position. But she also knew that people's beliefs were hard to break down with debate, no matter the arguments made. She knew people like her ex-husband, and indeed other people, who would be defeated by the pang of human emotion. So she spoke again with a low, sad tone, as if she was speaking to herself. She said, "In a moment your children will come. You'll see how happy they are. They already have two children, with a third on the way. If you tell them that they are siblings, they'll certainly get divorced. If they understand and have faith like you, that's OK. But if they don't have faith, it'll break their hearts. It'll destroy their lives, lives you've already damaged. They'll divorce. Then what will become of their children? Three kids is no small thing. How deeply will they be wounded by the insults they'll get down through the generations? And the insults will hurt them. It'll be all right if they have faith like you. But if not?"

Iyah spoke for a very long time, slowly and with a tender but sorrowful voice. And during that time, without him being conscious of it, the edifice he'd constructed was being undermined.

"I know," Iyah went on, "that it's a great sin to not let them know that they are siblings. But I was wrong from the start. I found out too late about their blood relationship. That wasn't their fault. And as long as I haven't said something I've been oppressed with a feeling of having sinned all this time. But I've put up with that oppressive feeling for years. Up until now. Is my faith lacking, if my sins are my sins, and I won't share my sins with others, especially my children? It won't erase my sin to break their hearts and destroy their lives. As a man you have never felt the bitterness of life divorced from a husband. I have felt it. And I won't let Arni endure the same bitterness that I did."

But Iyah's voice was no longer steady. It had become hoarse and faltering. Then she sobbed. And at that moment the resilience of the edifice he'd constructed crumbled. He was beaten. Beaten by his feeling of humanity that clashed with his own faith in God. He took his cloth pack, then stepped towards the door. And before he closed the door again, he said wistfully, "Iyah, I shouldn't have come. In fact, faced with bearing the sins of these lives of ours, it would be better that we humans did not exist. But we humans still exist and God still exists, too. Sins against God will receive His forgiveness if we atone, Iyah, because God is merciful and gracious. But if the sins are against people, it is hard to resolve. And for a long time I haven't sinned against people, all the more so towards people of my own flesh and blood. I'm going, Iyah. And don't tell anyone about us, and about what we have done. You know what we have done, Iyah."

The woman nodded. Then the door closed very slowly. And the man calmly stepped forward, but his head hung low, like someone who has been defeated. And Iyah was left with a feeling that also went and disappeared in the distance, leaving behind the already closed door, because it followed her former husband, the father of Masri, and also the father of Arni.

A Wedding

What should he do with his heartache? He wanted to punch something with all his strength, strangle, berate, thrash whatever he could. He had actually already punched something. Punched the wall of the house to let out his heart's fury. He wanted to do it over and over again until his heart was satisfied. But he couldn't do that in front of his mother. Then he ran out of the house, making a bee-line for the shore of Lake Maninjau with its clear waters. Now he could still feel the pain in his knuckles. He had even broken the skin.

The placid atmosphere by the shore of the lake and a gust of gentle breeze brought him back to his senses. Now he felt funny because he remembered how his mother yelled his name, running to catch up with him, as though she was afraid that her child would kill himself by throwing himself into the lake, leaving the other people watching the scene flabbergasted. There were even some who tried to join in the chase. He had been really heartsick. So heartsick. And he ran in the direction of the lake not because he wanted to kill himself, but rather he ran to carry all the ache and sting of his feelings, just like Chairil Anwar had said in his poetry. Those verses that he had memorized, every one. It was odd, if someone thought that he would want to kill himself over the issue of a wedding.

This was no longer the age of killing oneself over a wedding. The age of moralistic, nationalist novels was long since passed. Especially for people like him, a campus activist on the front lines of fighting for truth, justice, and freedom—the activist most called upon and listened to by the government. He wasn't looking for death in that struggle, even though there was the risk of being shot by a stray bullet. How could he possibly want to die over the issue of a wedding demanded by his mother? He wouldn't even kill himself if he failed to marry Lely, his love, like he had promised her. That was when she doubted how faithful the love of this Minangkabau boy could be, because she knew that Minangkabau boys were more bound to their mothers than to promises of faithfulness to their lovers. He would be so disappointed if he failed to marry Lely, like Hamid in the novel *Under the Protection of Ka'abah* whose heart was broken because he couldn't marry Zainab. However, he assured Lely, if something went wrong, it wouldn't be because of him.

The day before yesterday he was still in Jakarta. He was preparing a speech for a seminar put together by an organization that he led. The topic of the paper they had asked him for was on inter-ethnic and interracial reconciliation to accelerate national unification. He accepted the theme not because his love, Lely, was Chinese-Manadonese, from the far corner of Sulawesi on the other side of the archipelago, as different from him as could be. Rather he accepted it because of his belief in the majesty of Great Indonesia, as Muhammad Yamin had praised in his sonnets.

While he was still wrapped up in writing the paper, there came a telegram from his village that instructed him to come home because his mother was gravely ill. Although he left behind his work in Jakarta with a heavy heart, he still went home. He didn't want to be caught out again as before, when there was news that his father was ill but he didn't go home. And ten days later, there came news that his father had died. He was so regretful and bitter at his own actions. He couldn't shake the feeling for months.

But just now, when he had reached his house, his anxiety was replaced by a stinging feeling. He didn't find a somber atmosphere, but a joyful one, as though there was going to be a party. At first, he imagined that his mother would be laid out in agony—all the relatives gathered together with their eyes swollen by tears or glazed over or sobbing, waiting for death to arrive. But what he found was not what he had imagined. His mother was still sitting calmly, just as before. Passing a quid of betel nut from the right side to the left side of her lips. She was still in good health. She sat overseeing some women hanging wedding decorations in the living room. And when he arrived, his mother had no reaction at all. It was as though her child had come back from visiting the house next door.

Lumbering like a water buffalo who'd had too much to eat, his mother got up from where she was sitting on the floor. She brought him to his room. His heart began to race as though the story of Sitti Nurbaya—that ill-fated young woman forced into an arranged marriage in the classic novel—could be happening again. And he was the one who would be made Sitti Nurbaya himself. A college-educated man. Could this happen to him now? Even though he knew that there were still many young men who graduated from university and were forced to marry by their mothers, he never thought this would happen to him. But why was he sent a telegram to come home because his mother was gravely ill, when the house was being decorated for a marriage? Who was going to get married? Him?

"Sit over here, Ismet," his mother said as she swept up pandan blossoms with a broom, when Ismet asked who would be getting married and why he was instructed to come home.

"You're not ill, are you, Mother?" Ismet asked again.

His mother just kept on sweeping the floor mats.

"I am really busy with my duties in Jakarta, Mom. Why was I instructed to come home using a lie?"

"Actually we wanted to tell you a long time ago. But we thought you were busy with your exams. We didn't want to bother you. We were thinking this would happen next year. But your Uncle Adang, the man responsible for you in our culture, is going to Mecca this year, so the arrangements had to be moved up. That is the reason you were instructed to come home," his mother said.

"Why did you have to use a telegram that said what it did?"

"So you would be sure to come home, child."

"Why did I need to come home?"

"Your Uncle Adang wants your wedding to happen now."

It was like a bomb exploded when he heard those words. And he was heartsick to have been treated like a child in this way. A child who did not have any choice, could not question the wishes of his parents. He looked at his mother with eyes full of heartache. His heart was like the heart of a woman looking at someone torturing her baby. His face became flushed and he started sputtering. He cursed himself for being so stupid, for letting himself be tricked. It was as though he forgot that he was facing the woman who gave birth to him twenty-six years ago. The mother who struggled so hard to give him a life after his father was struck by years of paralysis that eventually took his life. All the women that were in the house were speechless, even afraid, when they heard Ismet holler like he had been possessed by an evil spirit.

At that moment, Datuk Bareno, the older brother of his mother, the man whom Ismet called Uncle Adang, arrived. Maybe someone told him that Ismet was acting like someone possessed by an evil spirit. His uncle had once been a man of high rank. Rich, too. He owned swaths of paddy fields in several different villages. His character was the kind that it was hard to disagree with. But all the local people deferred to him and respected him because he was quick to help others and cared about social needs more than anyone else in their village. Ismet respected him a lot, too. Not because this was his uncle and guardian, but rather because of all the help he had had given Ismet to continue his studies. If Ismet asked, he was almost never turned down. This uncle was also the main support for the needs of his mother and younger siblings.

Ismet didn't care about the arrival of his uncle. On the contrary, he poured out his anger at him. He ranted and raved. He wanted a strong reaction, so there would be an altercation. But the old man did not react. He let Ismet release all his anger and fury and rage. And when Ismet was out of words, only then did the old man start to speak. He said, "If you want to continue to be stubborn, go ahead. The plans for your wedding can be cancelled. The bitterness of being insulted by all the people who have been invited, I will carry that burden. But let me remind you, in that case our bond would be broken right here and now. You would have to look after your own mother and all four of your siblings. You would have to leave this house and go back to the house you came from. As your uncle and guardian, I will give you two days to think this whole thing through, son. I'm not marrying you off to just anyone, but to your own relative, my daughter Hasni, the ideal match in our culture. Do you hear what I'm saying? I will not fight you over this. I only want one thing: that you do what we want."

When his uncle had gone, Ismet punched the wall of the room with his fist while crying out as loud as his voice could carry, like a karate-master making his move. Then he ran out of the house. From the stairs he tumbled onto the ground. The women who saw him shrieked. But Ismet picked himself up. He ran in the direction of the lake. He paid no attention to his mother crying out in worry.

ങ

The clear water of the lake had little ripples, the tiny fish in the lake looked like they were swimming carefree, and these just compounded his feelings because he felt so jealous, to the point where he was still gasping for breath, even more than he had been gasping after running to the lake shore. He felt like he had lost all room to maneuver and decide on his position. He became starkly aware that this was the moment that would most determine his future. Maybe this would have a greater determining impact on his life than his final exams, he thought. If he made a mistake in setting his course now, his whole future would become muddled. A wedding should not become a reason to bulldoze his aspirations. There were plenty of people who were successful after they married, even after they had lots of children. Because a wedding was not a major event in the life of mankind.

However, a wedding that was forced by parents on the children was a strange event—it could even be counted as crazy if this tradition was allowed to continue on unabated. Forcing a wedding on children, what's more on children who were well-educated, was like throwing a wrench in the works of history's forward progress. Even crazier if that wedding was between two close relatives. Biologically this could lower the quality of their offspring. Psychologically it could hamper the quality of the marriage, because their attitudes and worldviews would be dammed up by a stagnant, traditional bond. Sociologically this could contribute to exclusivism. Politically it would inhibit feelings of national unity.

In his paper on the subject, he placed special emphasis on the main theme of building a path of renewal for Indonesian national unification in the future. But now he himself felt forced to marry Hasni, the daughter of his uncle and the member of the family to whom he was closest. If he agreed to a wedding, that would be the same as betraying his ideals as a youth leader upholding the pillars of the state and hopes of the nation. It would betray the ideals of his friends in the fight. It would also betray his love for Lely. More than that, it would betray Lely's love for him. Where could he hide his face if he went back to Jakarta? What would the life they built be like moving forward? Who would ever trust him again?

If he refused a wedding with Hasni, what would happen? The world would not end. However, how would it be for his mother, if his uncle really did want to bring down the hammer? Would a rich older brother, someone with the title of Datuk, be able to stand watching his younger sister and her children left high and dry? Was Minangkabau traditional law really as harsh as all that, as implemented by a chieftain of the family, the responsible man of the longhouse and the uncle and guardian of these children?

Suddenly he felt that he had to speak with his uncle. He felt he had to put forward his principles as a young, modern man, living in a world that was ever smaller, where the relations between nations were like a big, worldwide family that could not avoid one another anymore. He also had to put forward what he had worked so hard for and built up for the future. How his friends of his generation lapped up his ideas and the national leaders looked to his abilities as part of a generation to carry their work forward, the foundation for building up the nation. If his uncle only knew how great and serious his struggle was, surely this problem of a wedding with Hasni would become unimportant. And the wedding would obviously throw everything he had gained so far up in the air. He would also say that he already had a girlfriend of three years. A young woman who shared his ideals, a relationship where they understood each other's attitudes and actions. For a man who has confessed his love to a young woman who was willing to wait for him for so many years, it was improper for him to drop her with no logical reason. For Hasni, there would be no shortage of men for her. If need be, Ismet could find a partner who would be a better fit for Hasni. He had plenty of friends who had made something of themselves in Jakarta.

"Uncle Adang, I want to tell you something," said Ismet when he came face to face with the man who was his guardian.

"Good," said Datuk Bareno.

Ismet worked to control his emotions as he put forward everything that he had been thinking about when he lost himself in thought at the lake shore, even as his hands gave him away by waving around to emphasize his points and certain words. Datuk Bareno listened, unchanging like a village headman from the old times listening to a report from one of his underlings. He almost didn't move at all. His two hands were on his hips. A sliver of his upper body was hit by the late afternoon sun, while the rest of his body was in the shade of the roof of the longhouse with its six points like water buffalo horns. The shadow of the palm-frond thatch on the ridge of the roof swayed back and forth across his plump belly.

"Uncle Adang," he continued, "do not treat me like a child anymore. I am an adult. Don't try to force me into anything anymore. I already have a girlfriend."

Datuk Bareno was stock still. As though he knew that his nephew still wanted to say something more.

"Uncle Adang, I will not marry Hasni. I will marry a woman who shares my ideals, to uphold a system of national unification. So that the next generation will not be riven by the plagues of regionalism, ethnocentrism or racialism. The Indonesian state must be founded upon one nation without any consideration of ethnicity, race, even religion. That is my ideology. I will not waiver from it."

After listening to all the arguments that Ismet put forward, Datuk Bareno began to inch forward slowly, until he was right in front of Ismet. And he stared into his nephew's eyes without blinking. He raised his left hand and placed it on Ismet's shoulder. Then he said, "Is that all?"

After Ismet restated his position with a few words while nodding, the Datuk picked up where he left off. "Look at this village, really look at it. This village is getting emptier with the passage of time.

The mosque, as big and fancy as it is, never gets full anymore. Sometimes we cannot even have congregational prayers on Fridays because the only preacher we have goes out to meet with his friends in other regions. There are more fields left fallow than plowed. Why? Because the village is emptier and emptier. The men are gone. The only ones left are old folks and children. The ones who are unproductive. And the children when they grow up, they head out to seek their fortunes elsewhere, too. Many of them get married out there. And then they never come home again. It keeps going on like this. Before too long, our village will be taken over by the forest again. But you, the young people of this age, you modern folks, have never remembered and never even thought about how it would be when every village is abandoned by its residents."

When Ismet wanted to speak, the old man kept on going. "You young people can have all the ideals you want for yourselves. But in reality, what will you get for them? Almost all of the great ideas you have as students you abandon as soon as you graduate. There are even plenty of folks who participate in the destruction of their very own late ideals as soon as they learn that life isn't easy. Go ahead and list down all your idols, the patriots from one generation to the next, whose names sound so glorious when you're a university student. Where are they now? What tiny proportion of them are still faithful to their ideals? How can you build a new world, if you don't even pay attention to the old world that is crumbling all around you?"

The Datuk didn't give Ismet the opportunity to speak. He continued straight on, "You think I am setting you up with Hasni because I want Hasni to get a partner who graduated from university? No, son. University graduates are a dime a dozen these days. It's also not because I have spent so much money to pay your tuition, such that I want to get a return on my investment. No, son. Paying for your tuition or paying the upkeep of your siblings is my duty—the duty of an uncle and guardian to his nieces and nephews, the duty of a chieftain to his clan, the duty of a man to his widowed sister."

Ismet let out a wail as he listened. And then the Datuk let go of Ismet's shoulder. "I am marrying you to Hasni with the goal that, no matter where you go to seek your fortune, your heart will still be stuck here in our home village. You will continue to think of it and help to take care of it, so it won't get emptier and emptier, it won't become more abandoned, so it won't be taken over by the forest or sold off to some outsider or foreigners. So, ... I have done this for an ideal that is no less great. I don't know if you would be happy to see this village taken over by foreigners and you become an outsider in your own land, such that the native residents live huddled under a bridge. It is as though you want to build a brave new world, but you want to leave your own nation to be displaced from under one bridge to under the next."

Looking into Ismet's eyes, he knew that his nephew still wanted to object. He immediately started talking again, "So many people from our village have gotten married far away. With our own people or with others. Only a very few of them still remember their home village. This despite the fact that so many of them have gotten so rich. Go travel around the Minangkabau homelands, you'll see just how much deprivation there is in the villages left behind by all their residents. How many houses are broken and falling down. How many mosques and prayer houses are standing unused. And the residents themselves are poor because they don't know what work they could take up."

The shadow of the longhouse roof that was previously up to his stomach was now covering his whole body. The day was turning toward dusk. "I am happy to hear that you have ideals. I am proud because your ideals are big and lofty. But I think, your concept to build national unity through inter-ethnic and inter-racial marriage is off-base. That's not what national unity is. America did not become big and prosperous because they married across their ethnic divides or between the different nationalities that became their citizens. The dozens of races and nationalities that live there also vary in the colors of their skin and in their religions, but they are not torn apart. You're off-base, son. Your concept is off-base. But it's no good for us to debate here in the yard. It's already dusk. Let's go inside."

ભ

In the living room, Ismet was left alone by the entrance. Datuk Bareno did not come out again after he had disappeared over the threshold of the central room. It used to be that Ismet was no stranger in this longhouse. He would often come calling if he was on a school vacation. But now he felt like a stranger. He felt ill at ease. Maybe because he was aware that Hasni was in the inner rooms, the young woman that would be married off to him. It had been five years since he had seen her. He tried to remember her face. Oh, she was some kind of ugly. Her hair was combed straight back and tied up like the tail of a goat. He compared her to the face of Lely, who was fair as could be. Although Lely was simple in her tastes, she was neat wherever she went. Graceful and energetic, but always joyful. Full of initiative, and never complaining.

"No matter what happens, I will not marry Hasni. This village won't fall apart over this one girl," he said to himself. Then he decided that the next day he would head back to Jakarta.

From the inner rooms he heard the sound of sandals shuffling closer and closer. He was sure that he would be face to face with his uncle again. He steeled his heart to put forward his position. And the shuffling of the sandals paused at the threshold of the door. Slowly he turned towards the door. Hasni was standing there.

Bowing. Her fingers intertwined. She looked like she had just bathed. Her face was plain with no make-up and no accessories. She was wearing a white gown with a pattern of little red and black flowers sprinkled across it. Her collar was open, as though it had been caught out by her two shoulders. This made her collar draw that much more attention. Her hair was combed tightly to the back and tied with a band at the back of her head, falling down in a ponytail. Ismet was struck with the sight of her for several moments. He had not imagined that in the intervening five years Hasni had changed so much, and now he had lost track of the time that he had stood awestruck at the sight of her.

Slowly, the young woman crossed in front of Ismet, who was still following her with his eyes almost unblinkingly. Slowly Hasni lowered herself into a chair. Then she lifted up her head and stared straight ahead without looking at Ismet who was sitting to her left.

It was ages before Ismet spoke. He said, "You know that I've been fighting with Uncle Adang?"

"I heard from somebody," the young woman answered in almost a whisper.

"You know what I'm fighting with him about?"

Hasni nodded.

"What do you think?"

The young woman inhaled deeply. Ismet waited a long time for the voice of the young woman. "I am my father's daughter. Whatever my father wants, I will accept."

Then Ismet talked for a long time. He explained again what he had told Hasni's father in the yard. But he did it calmly and gently. He also told how he had had a girlfriend for three years, and he couldn't possibly call that off. "No matter what, you are my young cousin whom I care for, just like before. And you have to understand what my difficulty is," said Ismet to finish his speech.

Hasni's head, which had been straight and stiff to start, began to droop when Ismet said that he already had a girlfriend. She took a good while before she began to speak. She said, "I have heard everything you said, brother. I understand your situation. I also have ideals, even if they're only little ones. I also have yearnings. I have hopes. I also have a heart that can love and be loved. But before I take a step, before I make a decision, I take account of my position first. I weigh everything from the perspective of the people I love. So, before I am carried too far along by my emotions, I hush them up. So that there will be no conflict between me and my father or anyone else. I know what Father has done for us. Because of all he has done, we all respect him. It never crosses our mind to reject something that Father wants. Because there really is no use."

She wiped away the tears rolling down her cheeks with her pinkie finger. Then she continued, "You, brother, can do whatever you like, because you are a free man, a man who runs his own life. But me, I'm a person who is dependent on someone else to provide for me; I cannot be like you, brother. You're a person who is free. A person who has no debts of any kind to anyone. Of course, you can turn down a wedding because you feel like you're being forced, but I cannot."

The young woman stood up. Then she looked at Ismet. "You can dislike me, brother, and say horrible things about the plans for this wedding. But I have no reason to oppose my father's wishes. Because my father has done so many good things for me." After saying that, Hasni walked right out without taking her leave of Ismet.

Unconsciously, Ismet walked out the door of the longhouse and down the front stairs. And with each step towards his mother's home, it was as though his feet were weighed down by the echo of Hasni's final words. "You can dislike me and say horrible things about the plans for this wedding. But I have no reason to oppose my father's wishes. Because my father has done so many good things for me." And the end of the sentence echoed back at him: "Father has done so many good things for me. For me. For me."

And then, as he passed through the yard of the longhouse, a water buffalo who was tied up in the grass looked at him. Then it mooed as if begging for its life. It was as if it knew that life would last only one more day.

The Two of Them

Does regret lighten one's grief? Does regret bring back life that was lost? It is regret that squeezes cries out of the corner of your heart, and makes tears gush out. Basri didn't cry from the endless regret. But his heart was still crushed, so much so that his whole chest felt clenched, and he felt the pain. He didn't cry like Sutinah, who was wailing. Even though his heart wanted to howl, too, to express his sadness that was no less than the sadness of his wife. Maybe even more. After all, wasn't the man in the emergency room his own father? The man who died after being hit by a recklessly driven city bus?

"It's OK, dear. It's OK. It's better that we think of Papa's burial," said Basri in the pauses between his wife's crying and sobbing. But those words felt to Basri as though they were from the voice of someone else, someone who had come to comfort his heart's suffering. And he felt comforted. Sutinah even stopped her sobbing. She wiped her tears with the end of her headscarf. Then she looked into her husband's eyes with a look that asked for more words of comfort to persuade her.

"We can bury him in our yard, dear. So every day we can visit the grave. The grave we'll cover with marble. We'll get a decorative iron gate," said Basri.

"On the fortieth day we'll have the ritual meal. We'll ask an imam to come lead us in prayers so Papa's soul will go straight to heaven."

"Yes. Of course." Basri fed her yeses.

"On the hundredth day we'll have another ritual meal."

"Yes. Naturally."

"And then on the thousandth day. Right, honey?" After Basri nodded, Sutinah said again, "We'll find a famous artist. We'll have him enlarge Papa's portrait. We'll put it in the center room. Right, honey?"

Then they were both silent. The beautiful plans lifted up their hearts, as a balance to the regret of Basri's father's passing. Sutinah didn't cry any more. And she sat on the white bench next to the emergency room and didn't go in with her husband again.

For almost three full years she had been persuading his father to come live together with them. All that time her father-in-law had turned her down. Who knows why? Maybe it was because of leaving behind his house and the fields he had bought with the money he'd saved up little by little. Maybe it was the sweet companionship of friends his own age who went to and came home from the mosque all together. Or more likely it was because he was chairing a committee to build a school. If he left, surely the school would never be finished, because he was the one whom people trusted with their donations.

"I want our village to be as advanced as any village. I want the kids in our village to be as advanced as the kids in any village," wrote Papa in one of his letters.

Because a letter came from Basri that was a little too long, he finally agreed to come and visit for a month or two. Not to stay, he insisted. He would come after harvest. He would take on the journey just as Basri planned it out, so he would not get lost. Basri and Sutinah would pick him up at the train station.

But on the day that his father was coming, Basri and Sutinah woke up late. The night before, they had stayed up and talked the night away at his boss's son's circumcision party, until it was too late.

Basri was ready first, and had long been ready to go to the station, while Sutinah was still choosing the clothes she would wear. She paid no mind to her husband complaining up and down. "From last night I already told you: 'Don't cook beforehand; we'll be late.' But you just had to cook."

"If Papa gets home, what were you hoping to give him to eat? Air?" asked Sutinah.

"I hope he hasn't worn his eyes out looking for us."

"Don't worry, honey. Trains are usually one or two hours behind schedule."

"If they're late, sure. But what if it's on time?"

"When has anything ever happened on time in our country, honey?" asked Sutinah as she straightened her *kebaya* which had just been decorated with new beads.

"For years we asked Papa to come visit, and when he finally comes, it's as if we don't care enough to welcome him. Now how do you think Papa will feel?" Basri kept complaining.

"If you were Papa, sure. But Papa isn't like you, dear," answered Sutinah.

Basri still complained. "If this is how women put on clothes, how can the world advance if a woman becomes president?"

To stop his complaining, Sutinah asked: "Is the car all ready, honey?"

"You're the only thing that isn't," answered Basri. Aggravated, he went out. He slammed the front door to release his aggravation.

But the aggravation didn't go away. In fact, it doubled when he saw his car tire was flat. His thoughts went every which way. Bouncing back and forth between feeling embarrassed at having barked at his wife for taking so long to put on her clothes and thoughts of how embarrassed he would be if she knew about the car. He raced to set up the jack. He raced to change the tire. The spare tire was not yet on.

Sutinah appeared at the doorway. Then she said: "What's going on with the tire, honey? Flat? Change it quick. Soon we'll be late."

"Yeah, yeah, yeah," said Basri, almost shouting.

"Hey, what the hell do you mean by that?" swore Sutinah.

Basri was even more aggravated. He fit on all the nuts quickly, then screwed them in with all his strength, as though he wanted to demonstrate just how aggravated he was with the whole mess.

From then on the two of them were silent. Basri sped the car along like he was drag racing. The wheels screeched at each turn and bend. He did this not only out of aggravation, but also out of his anxiety, because he knew the train's scheduled arrival was already a half-hour ago. Meanwhile Sutinah was silent from her fear of the disaster that might result from the crazy way her husband was accelerating the car.

And that disaster actually came, too, when Basri kept accelerating even though the traffic light had already turned red. The policeman watching the corner stopped them. After their business with the police was taken care of by handing over a crisp bill, Basri could keep going. But his watch showed that he was already forty-five minutes late. He had to step on the gas no less than before.

Sutinah wanted to tell him to just go slowly. Even if the train had already arrived, his father wouldn't go anywhere. He would wait for them on the platform outside the station. But she was afraid to speak. Another word from her might make her husband even more reckless.

Even far before the station they could see the telltale signs that his father's train had already arrived. Lots of cars were already coming out from the direction of the station. Even the pedicabs were jostling to come out. Both of them were equally uneasy that his father had had to wait so long. It would be a real problem if the old man had to take a taxi or pedicab because he thought he was not going to be picked up. Even worse, lots of taxi drivers were no good and took passengers for a ride around and around so they would get a higher fee. If his father took a pedicab, what if the driver did not know their neighborhood?

All of a sudden, from a distance, Sutinah saw an old man who looked like her father-in-law who was wearing a *peci* hat and a folded *sarung*, carrying a small suitcase. She squinted her eyes to determine whether or not that old man was her father-in-law. But the car just kept accelerating quickly, so she couldn't be quite sure. However, after a moment she almost screamed: "That's Papa."

Basri hit the brakes. The tires squealed against the asphalt of the road. "Where?" he said.

"There. Behind us."

Basri backed the car up. He stopped close to the old man. But the old man felt that his way was being blocked, so he walked around into the middle of the road.

"Papa," they cried, almost together.

Just at the moment they called out, a city bus passed, accelerating fast from behind. The old man was hit.

The crash threw him several feet down the road. Again they called together "Papa!" This time screaming.

"If I hadn't been so stinking slow about my clothes just now ..." said Sutinah, who felt horribly at fault for their being late to the station.

"It's not your fault. It's me. Why didn't I check the car tire earlier?" said Basri, who took all the blame on himself.

Both of them kept talking. They each took the blame on themselves, who was the cause of his father dying in the crash. They did this so much that people going back and forth in the hallway next to the emergency room started staring at them. They both felt like they were the only ones there, waiting for the doctor to finish examining the corpse. Waiting to bring it home.

Sutinah stopped grumbling to herself and was silent for a moment. Suddenly she said, "Honey, shouldn't we call the house, let the kids know we're here?"

Basri immediately stood up to make the call. Not much later he came back with hurried steps. "Quick, come on, we're going home," he said, tugging at Sutinah's hand.

"What's wrong?" asked Sutinah, whose steps were dragged along by the tug of Basri hurrying to go.

"Come on, get in quickly," said Basri, urging Sutinah into the car.

"What on earth is it?" asked Sutinah again after she had tumbled into the seat of the car, pushed by her husband.

"What on earth is going on to make you like this?" Sutinah asked once more after the car had made it out to the main road outside the hospital.

"That old man wasn't Papa," answered Basri.

"Huh?"

"Papa is at the house already. He took a taxi. It was him on the phone."

"What?" asked Sutinah, halfway between believing and not.

"Papa is at the house already. Waiting around at the hospital won't do any good unless we're looking for a job."

"What if the doctor comes looking for us?"

"Isn't that *his* business?"

"But wasn't it us that took him there just now?"

"I don't care. You're really not thinking straight," said Basri, half scolding.

And, accelerating the car to leave the hospital further behind, they left behind the corpse of an old man whom they had suspected was his father, whom they had cried over together with all the pain of regret.

An Interview

Once there was a journalist for the newspaper *World Trumpet*. His name was Wahidin, a thin fellow, with a flat ass and long hair, and he had just gotten the most esteemed opportunity that any journalist has ever gotten in the history of journalism. Wahidin was invited to attend a special meeting of all the most prominent and most acclaimed people in the world.

Thinking that the circulation of his paper would increase hundreds of times over, he boldly strode into an impressive building. His newspaper would surely take every corner of the world by storm on the basis of this special interview he was about to do. And his name as a journalist would be burned into the minds of every human being until the end of time. This interview would be his last interview ever, because after this he would be appointed as a diplomat to one of the biggest countries in the world.

But what happened was exactly the opposite. His desire to interview the most prominent people in this impressive building was cut off by his desire to spread news to everyone he met there. Because what he found inside that impressive building were none other than the prophets. And Wahidin the journalist felt he had to tell them the news of "The World Today," because he thought that would be a real surprise for them.

"Adam, sir," he said, "Did you know, sir, just how many millions of your descendants there are these days? Did you know there are billions? Your descendants, sir, are growing like bedbugs.

Even though they have been killed on a massive scale, they keep growing fast and furious. Just like bedbugs, they are rotten little bloodsuckers. Did you know, sir? Your children, sir, Cain and Abel became an example of how one brother could kill another. This classic example is still an illustration today. Everywhere in the world today it is brother against brother, civil wars as fierce as anything."

Next he directed his words to Noah. "You know, sir," he said, "how you once asked God for the end of the world? Now we do not have to ask God for the end of the world anymore. What's more, people in the world today reject the interference of God in their lives; they know how to destroy the world themselves. If it used to be that you, sir, made a boat when the floods came and put all the types of animals inside, what would you do, sir, if a nuclear bomb were dropped to bring the end of the world?"

The question went unanswered by Noah for a few moments. He looked at all of his colleagues. And then Wahidin the journalist looked at a big-bodied man, strong and solid.

"You look like the fellow who parted the Red Sea, no? Did you know, sir, that your feat has long since been surpassed by man? Now people can split a mountain in half, then use that split to channel water from one lake to another."

"Amazing," said Moses.

"Truly. The seas today are already engineered by man. Lakes are dried out. On the engineered seas people put up buildings as tall as the clouds. And in the dry lakes people plant rice."

"How phenomenal."

"Trains creep their way through mountains, pass through the seas under the ground like a worm," continued the journalist, piling on examples.

"And you, sir, you have such a sweet face; if I am not mistaken, you, sir, were chased after by Potifer's wife, no? My my, sir, if you were in the world today, dozens of film producers would be fighting to get you under contract. If you did just one film, sir, and then stopped, you would be sure to cause mass hysteria. Truly, sir. I'm not just saying that. All the women in the world would scream and cry for a new film from you, sir. If you died, all of them would cry inconsolably. They would do it not because of who you are, but because of how you look, sir."

"Why?"

"Because people who are handsome or beautiful are more memorable for folks than people with good morals. And your picture, sir, would be pinned up by every girl and young woman in their bedrooms. After looking at your face first, sir, only then would they be able to close their eyes at night."

"Is that the temperament of women these days?" asked someone. Wahidin the journalist looked at the man, then he was filled with the desire to say something to him. He said: "What would you say, sir, if I told you it was no longer just you who was born without a father? Right now it is very fashionable for children to be born without a father. Women get pregnant without having a man around. If today it were still like the times when you were born, sir, everyone would make a big deal out of it. But having children like that is not a problem for folks anymore. Children like that are raised in a nice building. And rich people compete to give a little bit of money to fund those children. If you were born today, sir, the people would listen to all of your judgments. And you probably would not be crucified, sir."

"We won't be pulled in by your joking, sir," said someone.

"Hello, sir, you must be Muhammad, yes? What would you say, sir, if I told you that women no longer have any shame? Are you surprised, sir? It is really true, sir. What you said about shame, it is not shameful to people nowadays. Women can be totally naked in public now. Of course, the young ones, sir. If an old woman did that, she would surely be thrown into an insane asylum. That kind of young woman goes out dancing, sir. All the men who see them have to empty out their pockets. This is like social work, sir. The young women get food, while the men get entertained. In the old days, only kings were allowed to entertain themselves that way, sir. Now everyone can do it, sir. What, do you not believe me, sir? At the very least, lecherous men are calling for young people to live healthily. Then they build a swimming pool. Then they encourage girls to go swimming there. They have the girls compete in swimming competitions. Up to now I still do not understand what is the use of encouraging girls to swim, if they are never going to sea to catch fish. And the old men are hungry to see the girls' curvaceous thighs. And when they go home they get angry with their wives. It is true, sir. There are even people who rent an island and live there in big groups without clothes, just like Adam and Eve."

"How vulgar."

"Vulgar, you say, sir? There is no definition of vulgar that fits. Everyone rejects vulgarity, naturally. But because the definition of vulgarity is not consistent, how can someone call something vulgar?"

"If we believe your explanation, sir, what are marriages like in the world today?"

"Marriages between people are no longer a major issue. Without marrying, people can live together and have children. You yourself, sir, already permitted a man to have up to four wives, no? Your permission is already antiquated. A man can only have one wife; any more than that and he'll be called depraved. But because the man is a kind of stud, he can mess around with all other women he fancies, as many as he likes. That is what we call modern, sir."

"And do you, sir, approve of that kind of lifestyle?"

"Approve, you say, sir? If I approved, then I wouldn't have written in my newspaper that the ballet shows by the children of diplomats were vulgar."

"So what happened?"

"The diplomats got angry. I was brought before a judge. The judge punished me because he said I had insulted their honor. I was sentenced to a year in prison. But when I came out from the court, a group of people swarmed me, and beat me to death. Should we end things there, sir?"

"Good Lord," gasped several people almost at the same time. The sound was so loud that Wahidin the journalist was startled. And he woke up from his dream. And it just so happened that he heard the sound of a hard knock on his front door at the same time. He hurried out to see. There he saw several people in uniforms standing at attention, and one of them said very stiffly: "We have come to arrest you, sir. They were insulted with the use of the expression 'vulgar' about the social performance of the diplomats' children last night."

And wouldn't you know it, so the story goes, Wahidin the journalist met his end when he was beaten by the crowd as he came out of the court.

The Foreigners

Padang Panjang is a happy city. It's the city where I came into this life. For almost a fifth of a century it has continued to give me life. Indeed, the city does a lot to give life. There is the limestone that gives life. There is the river that gives life. There is the market that gives life. There are cars, there are trains that give life, although sometimes people also die having been flattened by them. There are many schools that give life. There are many soldiers, police officers, and their offices that give life. Although, during the revolution, many in the police and army took people's lives. The rain that falls a lot there also gives life, of course to the paddy fields and crops. The paddy fields and crops give life to people. The many shops also give life. And the houses lined up along the road also protect the people living there.

As far as I know, I have never seen a city that surpasses the city of my birth in giving life. Not Jakarta. Not Medan. Not Bandung, although that city is at the foot of a mountain, too. In those cities people live as if they are fighting for their lives. And their deaths are truly terrible, although with death their souls vanish as normal. It's also not like Denpasar, that city on the paradise island of Bali, because the paradise is just for tourists, but they also divide up penniless widows among themselves.

In the city of my birth no one lives like they are fighting for their lives. They live comfortably. They can walk about at ease, like water spinach brushed by a gentle wind. Every day, from morning till midnight, people can sit around or play cards in the coffee shops while drinking a cup of coffee on credit without getting sour looks from the owner. In the city of my birth indeed it's as if there is an excess of water, to the point that wherever we visit, women or girls hurry to prepare us a drink. The water in my city is not as wicked as the water in the River Musi or the Ciliwung, the rivers in Palembang and Jakarta. There aren't any floods. It doesn't carry along the carcasses of dead animals. Although someone once disappeared in a water channel, it was because he was struck by a fit, and the whole city was astir.

So that's the happy, life-giving city of my birth, which I left almost fifteen years ago, as fate willed that I live in another place.

Yet no matter how many people have left it, it is still a happy city. Many people have made their name there (and not always the name that they were given at birth). Islamic scholars from the whole of West Sumatra began building their fame there. They studied there initially, before their names were mentioned across the archipelago as major figures of our homeland. Despite this, people in the city of my birth were not preoccupied with putting up monuments. It's a good thing, too, since these days people put up monuments just like printing propaganda leaflets.

Truly the city of my birth is a happy city. Although the city didn't develop quickly like other cities, it still managed to develop, albeit slowly. Especially recently, there are more foreigners. Among these foreigners are Indonesians as well. Born in the city of my birth, they studied for a year or two abroad, and now they've come home. It's true that in the past there were already foreigners in the city of my birth, but most of them had joined the crew of a ship or were adventurous types who, disappointed with life, travelled to Malaya. Sometimes their wanderings took them to Mecca, and they would return with a turban. Of course, they did not make much of an impression on the city, because they did not go abroad to obtain anything. Certainly, several people went abroad to study. When they came home they had memorized the verses of the Quran and the Hadith. Then they became prominent leaders throughout the archipelago.

But since prominent leaders are no longer produced abroad, since the parties in Jakarta can now manage to produce them, the foreigners give rise to other hopes. Hopes that arise from the desire to gain practical knowledge for a new kind of life. So, looking to these foreigners who have just returned home, the city of my birth awaits a historic change as glittering as the past but in a new form.

Are those hopes going to be fulfilled with their homecoming?

I have only heard the story from my cousin. He is a person singular in his temperament and character, and his story made me smile.

The story went like this: You know Bahrum, don't you? Bahrum, the child of Uncle Jaya who has a food stall by the station? He went to Europe. He got a study grant—for five years. After he left, although he was far away he was always in our thoughts, and we talked about him a lot. We were proud that he was in Europe. Of course we were, you know? Since he is our friend, a close friend. All the more so back during the war. And if one of us got a letter from him, we would carry it around for days. Wherever we went, we would take it with us. Just like it was an amulet with supernatural powers. We would always show it off to everyone, and people would admire us. Or people would envy us, because we had a friend abroad. We really enjoyed it.

At some point our sense of pride slid away, like the snow sliding off a mountain peak when the summer arrives. We couldn't brag that our friend was abroad. Just like when snow melts to become water, then stagnates in a swamp, the same happened to us, to the point that we didn't dare show off the letters that came from Bahrum. The sun that came and melted the snow on the peak of our mountain of pride was someone who had just returned from abroad. He had been in America for a year. He was not our friend, but he, too, came from the city of our birth.

He was so very well-dressed. All his clothes were wool. He wore a bow tie, with a different pattern each day. He also had a hat and a big coat. And over his shoulder was slung the strap of a small camera. He took one step at a time, and with each step gave a nod of the head. If you considered how dashing he was, well, we were like little chicks cheeping between our parents' legs when a bird of prey was in the sky. And if he passed by while we were in a group, all our laughter would vanish. And without thinking, our heads would turn as if the angel of death had passed close by. But our eyes would be drawn round to follow him, accompanied by a feeling of envy.

Every evening, every morning, where there were crowds of people, he would surely pass by at certain times. His father followed behind him. When his father met people, he always greeted them with a smile while introducing his child: "This is my child. From abroad. From America."

Then he would leave them with their mouths agape.

And what really hurt us was that our sweethearts would also talk about the American every time they opened their mouths. All their praise was no longer for God, but for that American. And that meant that every reproach, every nag was just for us. We, who year after year as long as we'd lived, only knew how to hang around our mothers' kitchens.

When it was heard that the American was looking for a wife, those of my friends with pretty sweethearts became nervous. And all the girls busied themselves powdering their faces and putting on lipstick. And with all brand-new clothes they went out constantly. Rudely, if they met us, they didn't want to speak with us anymore. And definitely not go around together as a couple. Even if just by coincidence we were going the same way. We knew what they were up to. Of course it was so the American didn't think they already had a partner. And if the American passed by their houses, they crowded forward, sometimes even up to the gates of their house. Then, with a voice as sweet as molasses, they'd tell him "Drop by soooon."

Really our lives were adrift at that time. It was like fish whose pond has been poisoned with chalk.

He couldn't even speak the local Minangkabau language well anymore. He just spoke in Indonesian. Even to the old folks in the village. Sometimes it was mixed up with English: "Heyu. Kemon." Or sometimes we would hear, "Oke boi." Even to the old folks he would often say "Oke boi." We were shocked—the nerve of it.

One day another sun rose, such that from our viewpoint the American who had been like snow on a mountaintop now melted to water, weeping down like puss coming out of an ear. This sun was another foreigner. He came from Europe. Two years he had been there—so a longer time.

You must be thinking, he was more dashing, right? Yes. He was more dashing. Besides all the finery that the American brought, he also brought a scooter. Lambretta was the brand. Like the American who always accompanied by his father, the scooter roared around every afternoon and morning. The sound drowned out the admiration people had had for the American. Besides a tie and hat and coat, he also wore gloves. White gloves. If he greeted girls only then would he take off his gloves. Of course he did it so he could feel the softness of the girl's hand, I thought. But then he said it was etiquette.

Of course now you're thinking he was twice as stuck up, aren't you? Well he wasn't. He was really down to earth. To the point that he was indecisive and sometimes it was as if he let people walk all over him.

He became our friend. He always liked to come to the stall where we usually passed the day. And he would chat with us. He talked a lot.

He would have liked things better if he'd just kept his eyes closed. If he saw one of our particular mannerisms, then he'd say, "It's not like that in Europe." He'd see a muddy road, then he'd say, "It's not like that in Europe." If there were lots of flies he'd say, "It's not like that in Europe." If there was a scrum of people trying to get on a train or buy a cinema ticket, he'd say, "It's not like that in Europe." If he saw naked children in the rain, he'd say "It's not like that in Europe." He compared everything to Europe. But these stories didn't really interest us that much. And he himself preferred to talk about European women. And these stories made us want to go to Europe, too.

You know what he said about them? He said he'd been to Scandinavia. He said that there you could just embrace the girls if you wanted. And whispering he said, "Do you know, in those countries there's not a single girl who's a virgin?"

"Huh? If that's true, it's only the girls here that are born with a hymen?" we asked in surprise.

"Oh, no that's not what I mean. They easily give their virginity away," he said seriously.

"How do you know?" we wanted to know.

He just laughed.

"Have you tried?" we asked again.

He laughed again. But our question remained just a question. Because then he started talking about the girls in Holland. And those in Paris. Yet others in Rome. And the stories made us drool.

"And in Napoli," he said further, "you can hire a hotel room for 1000 lira a night. Complete with a woman to sleep with you."

"Whoa, man. A thousand a night?" we said surprised.

"In Jakarta 100 rupiah would be pricey," said another of us.

"1000 lira is only ten rupiah. And with a figure like Gina Lollobrigida."

We were really happy hearing his stories like this one. Because of the stories, we became more and more enthralled. It was far more interesting than the pornographic stories the police banned.

But the European was also really tight with his money. However much we chatted at the coffee stall, it was like he was allergic to paying for a round. It was always us that had to foot the bill. But we always liked him. It wasn't just that he had stories that made up for it, he was also very respectful towards us. If one of us went to take a cigarette, he would act in a flash. He would take the cigarette for us, then present it respectfully, and then he'd light our cigarette. And conversely, if it was us that presented the cigarette, and then lit it too, he would always nod and say thank you. He said that this too was the European etiquette.

But when it came to this I was actually really rude. If I wanted to smoke, then I'd say, "Sim, I want a smoke."

"Oh," he'd say. And quickly he'd present me with one, then light it as well.

"Thank you," I'd say, imitating his low voice and his showy mannerisms.

Seeing me do this too often, my friends did the same thing. So the European was constantly serving us up cigarettes and lighting them. But if it was just us there, we would just do as we did normally, taking them ourselves and lighting them ourselves. In the end he knew that we'd only adopted the European etiquette superficially. And he felt that we were making fun of him. So he didn't want to do it anymore. So he returned to being pure Minangkabau.

If he spoke with us, he always spoke calmly. Never in a rush, but rather one word at a time. And he would never speak over someone. If he wanted to interrupt, he would always say, "Wait a moment. May I interrupt?" Or sometimes he would say, "Excuse me. I'd like to speak."

But I was rude here, too. I imitated him in this, too. And my friends did the same. Saying the words one by one and at a measured pace. And if we wanted to interrupt, we said, "Wait a moment. May I interrupt?" Or we said, "Excuse me. I'd like to speak." But we would mostly do it if he was around. And if it was just us, well, we would just act like local folk. Disorderly. Whoever had a loud voice, they would be heard. They would win out. Eventually he started acting like a local again, after realizing that we were mocking him a lot.

One day he said that he had already carried out our people's revenge against Holland.

"How?" we asked all at the same time.

"I berated the Dutch in their own country. I ordered them about like a servant. Pick that up. Take this, widening my eyes and pointing with my left hand," he said, imitating the movements of a master berating his servant.

"Who was it that you scolded? Queen Juliana too?" we asked further.

He was momentarily speechless, and his eyes spun, lost for words as he looked at us.

"Surely it was just servants, wasn't it?" we asked again.

"Even if it's just servants, they were still Dutch after all," interrupted another.

"But the Dutch berated our leaders, while our leaders were treated like messenger boys," said another.

And in the end our conversation became merry and we cracked up with laughter. Meanwhile the voice of our companion who'd spent two years in Europe was silent. And from then on stories of Europe no longer reverberated in our ears.

However, new questions emerged in our hearts. What would Bahrum's attitude be like when he came home later? We'd already seen how stuck up someone who'd been abroad a year was. We also knew how showy someone was who'd been away two years. And Bahrum was abroad for five years. If not five times the American, surely he'd be at least twice the European in all his manners and influences.

Once again we talked about our friend. But we didn't talk about his letters any more. Because now we felt that there was no content to the letters besides menacing stories. We now only thought about what kind of showiness we would see later. The closer it came to his homecoming, the more often we talked about it.

And we were in agreement that Diah, his fiancée, a girl who was already twenty-eight years old, would have waited in vain. Now her body had become skinny. But she was getting more and more fair— because she no longer went out in the heat of the sun, and carefully applied her face powder thickly. However, she also became more and more skillful. She joined all kinds of courses. From sewing, darning and embroidery, to decorating flowers and doing make up. And it seemed as though news of her skill in cooking spread from the West, via India then to the Far East. Meaning that surely she wanted to position herself as Bahrum's angel. But she didn't know that Bahrum's angel could dance naked in front of a crowd in Europe. And of course Diah never got a letter that included stories about that European angel.

Finally Bahrum arrived. Our suspicions all that time completely missed the mark. Only one of them didn't, that being about Diah waiting in vain until she was twenty-eight years old. Just as soon as he got off the ship and met Diah, whose eyes shone with a hunger for his love, Bahrum only said, "Oh, it's Diah."

When Bahrum came home, he was just like when he went away. In fact, he had wool clothes too, but the wool was coarse. His socks were worn out, like his shoes were worn out. And his heart was still the heart of Bahrum of old. Although there were differences. They were even in his way of speaking. He also brought some European etiquette, and besides this etiquette he also brought a scooter. Also a piano and a radio with a record player and a tape recorder. Not forgetting a typewriter and a camera.

Yes. Certainly, he was humble and didn't put on airs. My thinking is that this was because he's an artist. He studied music there. Mainly the violin. And we figured that surely he was really already as great as Jascha Heifetz or Yehudi Menuhin, while he often used to say that he was the Indonesian Yehudi Menuhin.

Of course, we really wanted to hear the delightful sound of him drawing his violin bow. Even more so how the fingers of his left hand danced upon the strings. Would they now be as fast as the tongue of a thirsty snake? And his violin was truly fantastic, made from wood that was three hundred years old.

So one day, when there were no longer people thronging to visit, we came. We didn't come to hear more stories from overseas, because stories from overseas would be just like anyone's stories. We just wanted to hear him play the violin.

"Rum, play won't you," we said. "We really miss hearing you play."

He just smiled. Only after we pressed him again did he go to his room. We thought surely he would fetch his violin. And we were delighted. But when he came out he was only carrying a tape recorder. And when the tape recorder started, we could hear the sound of a violin with the accompaniment of a piano. Then he listened to it intently. The sound just went *eek aak eek aak* And we didn't understand. And we didn't feel its beauty.

"Is that you playing?" we asked.

"Is the one on the piano you as well?" asked another.

Then he said, "How could a person play the violin at the same time as the piano?"

"Les Paul supposedly can. He plays the guitar, he plays the ukulele and he also plays bass. His wife sings four voice parts. Why can't you, if he can?"

"It's a young woman playing the piano," he said, answering our question.

"Your fiancée, eh?" we asked irreverently.

And he winked. Then he told us about all his plans for the all things that he brought.

"I want to investigate the music from our region. Folk music in our region is no less beautiful than European folk music," he said.

Then he spoke for a really long time about the plans he'd long been thinking about abroad. He also told us about the songs of the Spanish Moors. About the polkas in Eastern Europe. Then black music which has permeated the souls of young people around the word. We just nodded, listening to him while our mouths hung agape.

"The piano that I brought is for arranging the music that I research. The tape recorder is to make copies of the original songs in the villages. The camera is for photo documentation. The typewriter, of course, is to type up the results of my scholarly research about the region's music. And the record player is to elevate the tastes of our musicians here," he said.

Whatever the hopes that he passionately described, in our hearts there also pressed a curiosity about how skillfully he'd play the violin after his fingers had been tempered for five years in Europe. Our curiosity grew. And finally we pressed him to play the violin made from three hundred-year-old wood. Finally he played, after he could no longer brush off our pressure. But the tune went *eek aak eek aak* like the sound the tape recorder made earlier. Then we asked him to play the tune "Sailing," because that tune was closer to our hearts. And, of course, we thought that he would play it more sweetly and serenely. Understand that his fingers had for five years been tempered by an Academy of Music.

"If that's really the way that you play, Taik's grandad could surely become a professor of violin in Europe," we said when he'd finished.

We were amazed that the foreigner had become awkward playing his ancestors' music. It was a waste, him spending five years studying in Europe. It would have been better if the government had used all those tuition fees for eradicating poverty.

And hearing our comments, he seemed really hurt. To the point where to this day we've never heard him play again.

After that he seldom met up with us. The reason, he said, was that he was busy. But soon after, he went to the government office in Bukittinggi. We thought initially that he was asking for a job, and we were surprised: why would a violin player ask for an office job? But it seems he was planning to set up a music school. The government agreed and asked him to draw up plans. Day and night he worked drawing up those plans, to the point that he looked pale and thin. When the plans were finished, he submitted them to the government.

"What kind of plans are these?" said the government official. "Where is the budget for staff? Where is the budget for constructing the building? How can a school be established if there is no building?"

"What's important is not the building, but rather the plan for the school," said Bahrum.

"Yes. The school is a building, isn't it?" said the government official, not wanting to accept defeat. "The plan is not up to scratch."

And since that moment, he no longer occupied himself with government offices. And his face was always creased in a sour frown and his heart overflowed with resentment. All the more so when the government officials kept sending him letters, telling him to immediately take up a position as a civil servant in the government office, as a fulfilment of his obligation as a scholarship recipient.

"I'd rather go to jail," he said frowning. Then he said to us, "If I sell all the things that I brought with me, how much do you think they'd fetch?"

"The piano and record player?" we asked surprised and hopeful, because we also wanted to help him sell them, since we worked as brokers.

"What about everything?"

"The violin too?" we asked.

"Yes, the violin too," he said firmly.

Now we were even more surprised. Then we asked further, "What do you want to do then?"

"I want to buy land. I want to become a farmer. It's better," he said.

How can that be, we thought, he'd spent so long learning music, in Europe moreover, and now he wanted to become a farmer.

And ever since then we only heard complaints and resentment overflowing toward everyone. Just like the way the American had behaved, when every day he complained because he couldn't go dancing. And the one who'd been in Europe for two years complained as well, because he didn't have money. After complaining, they criticized. After criticizing, they cursed.

We didn't understand at all why they were like this. After all, according to the elders' saying, if a young person knows the village loves them, they should go off to seek their fortune. But perhaps the people who came up with the saying were wrong. Because if people went off to seek their fortune in the past, they didn't go abroad.

In the end all the people who'd graduated abroad left, but their leaving was different from the leaving of the Dutch and the Japanese, who were truly pure foreigners. They left with sad hearts because of leaving our prosperous and tranquil Indonesia. Whereas these home-made foreigners left because they resented and cursed their homeland. Isn't that strange?

And the American, after studying agricultural science in America, now works in an office. Writing letters at the Ministry.

And when he started at the Ministry, he mortgaged out his parents' rice paddy too. And Bahrum, who studied arts, prefers to be a farmer. Only Kasim is different in his position. He studied graphics in Europe. And now he works in Kebayoran printing money. Whereas his parents' print shop is run by newcomers. But that's OK, since once he's an expert in printing lots of money, surely he won't complain about not having enough money anymore.

These home-made foreigners are strange, don't you think?

An Ideal Match

If the number of women were greater than the number of men, and the labor market shrank such that unemployment soared, it would not be hard to find a girl to become one's wife. Especially a girl who was already twenty-five years old or more. Because, as a spinster, society still sees them as worrisome individuals for their families. It's as though a spinster becomes a living blemish embodying the sins of the family. As a result, bachelors who had hit about thirty years old and were employed, like Badri, if they wanted to point their finger at those girls, then one would become his wife.

In a few more months, Badri would reach an even thirty years old. Compared to his classmates, he was already seen as seriously late in finding a wife. It wasn't because his pointer finger was crooked or mangled, but rather because of his far-reaching idealism in the social and cultural fields. When he realized that this struggle would not end even if he continued to live as a bachelor, still it wasn't easy for him to get himself a wife.

There were three kinds of hurdles that were not so easy for Badri to overcome as he thought all this through. First, so his descendants in the next generation would not be so short in stature, he hoped for a girl who was tall and slender. At least 160 centimeters tall. And that wasn't easy to find in a population that tended towards short. Another hurdle was that Badri was an ethnic mix, which was seen as not so appealing according to Minangkabau culture that preferred to marry within the ethnic group. Another hurdle was his calculations on the cost of living, where he would not quite break even if he got married.

According to his calculations, after paying for the cost of food and rent and the cost of his cigarettes, by the fifteenth of the month his pocket would be totally empty. Of course, following his logic if he lived as a couple with his wife, by the first of the month his pocket would have developed a hole. According to his more frugal calculations, the amount of his salary could feed one more person, plus buy a set of clothes for his wife once a year. But he would have to stop smoking, and he would only be able to go to the movies once a month. That wasn't a big deal.

The worst thing was when he thought about the consequences of the wedding. His wife would of course get pregnant and have a baby. According to his research, the cost of a single prenatal exam was equivalent to two days' salary. The cost of the delivery would suck up two months' salary. That doesn't even include all the expenses to buy baby supplies, from diapers and swaddling clothes to a crib. Badri concluded that he would never be able to get married. Unless he wanted to do what his co-workers did. Or like Mr. Mudo, the office gofer, who would do absolutely anything that the folks in the office asked him, above and beyond his office duties, in order to get compensation of various kinds, so that he could provide a living for his wife and their five children.

The other way out, according to Badri's thinking, was to marry a girl who had a job. The best thing was a girl who was a civil servant, because civil servants usually had a lighter work load compared to workers in private companies. The best kind of civil servant to marry was a schoolteacher, because schoolteachers were practiced in living very simple lifestyles.

Was there a girl whose height was around 160 centimeters, who was a teacher in a public school, and whose parents wouldn't mind a mixed-ethnic guy like Badri?

There actually was. Her name was Lena. She was four years younger than him. She was a girl who was so pleasant to be around that for Badri it felt like time flew while they were just chatting away. But each time Badri tried to escalate their friendship to the realm of romance by starting to ask her out to go to the movies, there was always a reason that Lena turned him down. Whether it was lousy weather, or bad movies, or feeling a bit sick, there was always something. Only once did Badri manage to take her to the movie theater. Even that was because he was accompanying her to take her two younger siblings who had just come from out of town. Even though he couldn't realize his hopes towards that girl, he would often go to visit her. And he always got a response that was warm and that never cooled off.

But then, there came a disaster.

One night, when Badri was visiting her again, Lena did not let him come in. Instead, she sounded like she wanted to drive him away, "Don't come back anymore!"

Badri was stunned to hear what Lena said. Even more stunned when Lena mentioned the name Rosni, a girl whom he often took out at night to go to the movies.

"I'm not serious with her," Badri said, pushing back.

"It must be nice to be a guy. You take a girl out at night all the time, but if another girl asks you about it, you can say that you're not serious with her," said Lena, cursing him in spite. And before Badri could give an explanation, the door was shut and locked from the inside. Badri was left stunned on the steps.

He trudged away from Lena's house, kicking himself for taking Rosni out all the time, even though that girl wasn't ideal for him. Sure, her face was pretty enough, with skin as clear as palm shoots because of her tender, young age, but Rosni was ten centimeters short of his ideal standard. Most importantly, she didn't have a job that gave her a living, and she was a bit too full-bodied.

From then on, Badri lost both girls who most pleased his heart. He began to avoid Rosni, because he didn't want to be bound up too much in mingling with her. And when Rosni married a guy chosen by her parents, Badri felt like he was out of the crosshairs. But on the other hand, each time he met Lena, wherever it was, the girl always turned her face away.

And in a few months, he would be thirty, an age where he was plenty ripe to become a husband, in his opinion. And he realized, too, if he didn't hold too tightly to his principles for living, he really could get married by his birthday. That was possible only so long as he was willing to accommodate himself to the conditions of society at the time. A small salary wasn't really a problem to cause a delay in getting married, because even with a small salary, plenty of people could afford to support three to seven souls. There were even plenty among them who became more prosperous the more children they had. Plenty of them, too, who had begun to build their own houses. It's not that Badri didn't know the way to increase his earnings. But, he thought, if I cannot help to improve the world, at least let me not make it any worse.

Although he had come to the conclusion that men were never too old to find their soulmate, every time he remembered his age was approaching thirty, he felt the push in himself again that he had to find a wife.

So he began to study the columns of personal ads, "Find a Match," that came out once a week in the newspaper of the city where he lived. He noted down all the girls who were looking for a match in the personals for three months' straight of printings. He made a table out of the notes with things like job, height, age, and other requirements. He found twenty-six bachelorettes and another seven who were widows. Badri wasn't interested in a widow. On the whole, the remaining candidates were over the age of twenty-four. And the most important thing was that all of them were employed. Nineteen of them were civil servants. Among those nineteen there were eight who were teachers. But only three of them were the height that Badri wanted. As it happened, none of them was averse to a match along the lines of Badri, meaning someone who wasn't a local boy. To pick one of them, Badri settled on a girl who had put an ad in the personals first. The girl's code was AX/19. So he wrote a letter immediately, asking the editor to put them in contact. The twelve days that he was waiting for a response were a kind of torture for Badri. But the five days before their first meeting, after they had been in correspondence, were even longer and practically suffocated him.

They were to meet in front of the Five Store at five o'clock in the afternoon. The girl would be wearing a yellow sweater with a violet skirt so he would recognize her, while Badri would wear a batik shirt and carry under his arm a magazine tied up with a red ribbon. Badri arrived five minutes before their agreed time, because he was afraid to arrive late. One minute before five, he was getting more and more jittery, with his wild eyes looking everywhere for a girl in a yellow sweater. Precisely at five, he couldn't take the torture of these jitters anymore. So he ducked into the shop with the intention to keep an eye out for the girl's arrival from inside the store. When he was just going in the shop's front door, a girl in a yellow sweater was just about to leave. They stared at each other in shock with eyes that were equally wide. Because that girl was none other than Lena.

But before Badri had a chance to think, Lena immediately turned away. With quick steps she passed right out of there, crossing the street. Badri quickly came to the conclusion that Lena must be his soulmate. This wasn't some random occurrence, but it was the pull of destiny. So he chased the girl quickly. And when he was close he grabbed Lena's arm tightly while matching her pace.

"Let go of me," hollered Lena as she tried to free her arm from Badri's grip. "I'll scream!"

Against all odds, Lena really did scream. People immediately came and crowded around them. It almost became a public incident. If a policeman hadn't come and broken things up, Badri would surely have been beaten up by the crowd. In front of the policeman examining them, all their cards were laid on the table.

"You're crazy!" said Lena, when she finished reading the manuscript of the short story that her husband had just written. "Are you really going to spill our story to the masses?"

Badri hugged his wife around the waist and laughed.

They had been married a long time, and now they had two little babies who had been born in quick succession. They had been married in a huge party that was celebrated in the Minangkabau traditional style. And since that time, Badri lived in the house of his in-laws, just like other husbands. The matrilineal lifestyle that Badri didn't like in his bachelor days, it turns out he didn't need to worry about it. The cost of living calculations that had bothered him so much before, it turns out he didn't need to think about them so much. What's more, when his second child was born, he recommended that Lena stop her work as a teacher. Because the art of life is not an exact science, but rather a process of adjusting oneself to the trends that are shaping society. And the idealism of his bachelor days turned out to just be a kind of utopia, that is, the idealism that infects people who don't have the burdens of family life. The idealism of a man who had become a husband and a father is an eternal idealism, namely seeking the ways to make his wife and children happy.

And if Badri occasionally read the newspapers that told the story of young people's struggle to reach their dreams, he would quickly fold up the newspaper and put it on the shelf with old papers, which his in-laws would later sell off secondhand.

The Water Buffalo Asks the Cart

Water buffalo once held a special meaning in my life for a time. But not because of the myth in *Cindur Mato*. That folktale tells the story of a magical water buffalo named Binuang, who had poisonous bees lodged in his ears that would come out and sting the robbers who disrupted their journey if the buffalo's master, Cindur Mato, so wished.

No, that's not why water buffalo held a special meaning in my life.

It's not because of the other myth, that tells about the defeat in war of a Javanese general fighting against the Two Great Datuks of West Sumatra, a defeat that happened when he lost in a proxy duel between water buffalos. The duel wasn't just messing around. If the Javanese general won, he could colonize the territory of the Two Great Datuks. But if he lost, he had to pack his bags and his whole army with him. In this fight, the Javanese general put forward a huge bull whose horns were long as a man's arm, he was so big. The Two Great Datuks put forward a bull calf that hadn't suckled his mother's milk for three days, so immediately he went to the hindquarters of the huge bull to suckle. Because they had rigged a big, sharp barb right on the snout of the calf, of course the big bull was gutted entirely from being cut by the barb. When he started running every which way, his body gave out and his soul flew up like a kite.

So, the Javanese general lost in the duel. Then he went back to his home empty-handed. On the other side, the Two Great Datuks,

Datuk Ketumanggungan and Datuk Perpatih nan Sebatang, who had won because they were so clever, they came to call their country after that episode. The name was Victory of the Water Buffalo, or *Manang Kabau* in the local tongue, which eventually became the word Minangkabau today. And since then, wouldn't you know it, water buffalos have become a hallowed animal. The head of the water buffalo put forward by the Javanese general was buried in the ground to ward off any more Javanese generals from ever coming again with the intention to pillage. Buffalo heads are even buried at the foundations of each building to keep the building safe from disasters. Or they are hung inside the house, to keep the house safe, too, from all kinds of dangers. Traditional longhouses are given sweeping roofs to look like water buffalo horns. And the owners of those houses, the women, fold their headscarves up on their heads into the shape of horns, and the headscarves are called horned veils. If disaster strikes—for example, if someone violates customary restrictions—the violator is sentenced to "a water buffalo's head," or to throw a meal for folks as a sign of repentance and slaughter a water buffalo. For the banquet of a big party, like installing a new chieftain, a water buffalo has to be offered up and its meat shared all around. The father's relatives at a wedding will give a water buffalo as a sign of pomp, and that water buffalo is paraded with a gong after being dressed all in yellow.

No, the myth of dueling water buffalos, with all its signs of greatness, is not why water buffalos held a special meaning in my life.

Even though that myth is believed and built up even to this day, still I get insulted if somebody calls me a water buffalo. I practically become a tiger to pounce on whoever calls me that. Unlike in the myth, a water buffalo as an animal is seen as pretty dumb. An animal without a whole lot of quality. Even though its power is strong to plow and pull a cart, its endurance goes right down as soon as the sun beats on it. In this way, it's inferior to the cow.

Wives prefer to make a curry out of beef rather than buffalo meat for their beloved husbands. And restaurants would all go bankrupt straight away if they used buffalo meat. And water buffalo hide isn't used for shoes, except the soles. And if you try to fry up water buffalo rind as a snack, it doesn't sell. However, its milk, sweet Lord, it is delicious, if it's fermented. More delicious than yoghurt. Even better if its covered with palm sugar, in a dish called *dadih*.

No, that's not why water buffalos held a special meaning in my life.

The special meaning in my life came because they often passed in front of my eyes. That was back in the days of the War of Independence. My father opened a little shop to change his profession, which for so long did him no good. My father's shop was located along the main road right in the middle of a long incline. It was smack in the middle of that uphill stretch.

Every morning and evening, if I didn't have anything else to do, I would go help my father at the shop. I'd clean the place up, or pack up what he sold. Usually I liked to work out on the porch. That way, as I was working, my eyes could scout around to watch the people passing to and fro on the main road. Of course, as a young man, the thing that caught my eye the most was young women. Even more so because lots of the young women of my town were good-looking. But in the end the thing that captured my thoughts the most was the carts and water buffalos passing by.

In the War of Independence, carts became a vital mode of transportation. Of course, not for carrying people, and especially not troops headed for the front. Rather, they were used for commercial goods, stuff like vegetables, cooking oil, soap or palm leaves and other things. Generally, the carts belonged to people living near the coast. They would leave the place they came from carrying coconuts, cooking oil, salt, soap whose tallow was made from palm rib ashes, palm leaves, charcoal. From my town people carried vegetables, lime for whitewashing walls, woven bamboo panels for house walls. So the carts were always full going and coming. It was all materials that had been ordered on a regular schedule from the two places that the carts visited.

Carts move really slowly. You have to understand, it's water buffalos pulling them. The distance between where they come from and my town can be reached in one day and one night. They would travel all together, between ten and twenty carts, like in a caravan. Each caravan came from a different village down by the coast. From the coast to my city the road was all uphill. Half of the uphill road was steep and wound along the sides of the mountain. A long uphill, and the steepest, was up the Anai valley. The drivers, who were called cartmen in my town, walked beside their carts that were filled extra heavy. They would have to take turns helping each other to turn the cart's wheels so it could go forward. At their stopovers every three or four hours, the water buffalos were set loose from their harnesses to feed and to ruminate. Especially when the sun was at its fiercest, when they would take longer rests. Where they stopped over there was always a place selling drinks. But the stopovers that they preferred were the ones that had cool fields. Not just because they were protected from the rays of the sun, but also because the ground was soft. And usually the stopovers were near flowing water.

Because the round trip took three days, the cartmen sometimes brought along their wives. Usually the ones they brought along were young wives whom they had just married. So the journey would be like a kind of honeymoon for them. If the wife came along, the cart's boarding, which was usually used as a place to sit or sleep during the journey, would be decorated with a sheet like a curtain in all kinds of tacky colors. They would also bring along a mattress and pillows. The lining and cover of the colorful sheet would be embroidered with floral patterns. The edges of the pillowcase would even have lace. So the boarding of the cart would become a kind of bridal suite.

I'm not sure exactly how romantic it is, the life of a newlywed couple on a cart. And I'm not sure how cheery the mood of the caravan is. But I can imagine a few things. At the very least, that situation would naturally whip up the hearts of the other cartmen to marry again with a young woman or a young widow. More than once in a while I saw caravans passing in front of my father's shop with women like that. Usually the woman's lips were reddened by chewing betel nut, as red as their fingernails that were dyed with henna, as a sign of their status as a new bride. Seeing something like that, I can draw a conclusion in my imaginings, that the cartmen must have been among the preferred men in their villages at that time.

The cart caravans from the coast always passed by my father's shop at the same time—in the late afternoon, the night before market, or in the morning of a market day. They went back on the afternoon of market day or the morning after. My town had market days twice a week, on Monday and Friday. The carts that would come in the afternoon would go back the next morning. The ones that came in the morning would go back in the afternoon. And each time they passed, no matter what, my eyes were drawn to them because of the cartmen, the water buffalos, and the carts themselves.

The cartman is a unique thing. His face is kind of smooth, but with a long mustache. His head is always covered with a woven hat that comes down like a face mask, the kind made from thick wool, like a skier's mask. The hat can be rolled up or pulled down to the point where it covers the whole head and only the eyes are visible. Their faces look fierce. At least they looked like that when they passed my father's shop. Their shirts were like Chinese-style button-ups and their pants looked like what you would wear for local martial arts. And their wide belts had little pouches on them. And each pouch had a snap to hold it closed. On their feet they wore sandals made of old tires, with thongs made from the rubber of inner-tubes. The carts were usually loaded up with cargo. Sometimes they overflowed the cart itself. To the point where the roofs stuck up like the hood of a car that's been propped open to fix the engine. But usually that kind of cargo was roofing made from palm thatch. And usually each cart from the coast would bring palm thatch as an extra burden. They would tether it to the tailboard. Sometimes, they would lash a drum of coconut oil to the tailboard. And if the tailboard was carrying a drum of coconut oil, then the cartman would sit on the front shaft of the cart, on a long trace that would hook onto the shoulders of the water buffalo. The reason for sitting there was to balance the weight during the long uphill.

Each trip up from the coast, each cart would stop a few moments in front of my father's shop. This was not to rest or because the cartman wanted to buy something from my father's shop. No, that wasn't why. The water buffalo would stop there to relieve itself, to shit. On the other hand, if they were headed home to the coast, they went by nice and calm. But as they went the water buffalo would piss. Shit and piss were always strewn in front of my father's shop, while I'd be there helping to clean the place up or wrap up what he sold. The water buffalos always did this right in front of my nose. And, because of that, my nose was always buffeted with the stench.

I got really cross. Why did they have to do that right in front of my father's shop? Was there no other place that was less crowded? Was that what the cartmen wanted? If they wanted it like that, what was it that made them dislike us, to the point where their animals would have to relieve themselves right there? It wasn't as though we had ever bothered them as they passed.

Lucky thing my town was a rainy place, so the filth and stench that the water buffalos left behind would be cleaned up naturally. But what if it wasn't the rainy season? At the very least, the water buffalo filth frequently caused accidents and was a pain for those who stepped in it, but a cause of laughter for those who watched. Accidents like that frequently happened at night. From the Japanese occupation, the roads in my town were usually dark at night, because the electricity wasn't switched on at the street lamps, both because of a lack of current and because the bulbs that had gone out couldn't be replaced or were stolen by folks. You have to understand it was wartime. These accidents were a bit as though the water buffalo droppings were landmines strewn over the road, so they would often take out the feet of passers-by. And every single time, there was a shriek whenever an accident happened. Of course, the styles of shriek varied. Imagine if an accident like that happened to a young bachelor who wanted to go courting at the house of his girlfriend, or a pair of young people who had just stepped out for the night.

I was resentful, but the accidents are not why. Instead, I was resentful because those water buffalos chose to take care of business in front of my father's shop.

One time I helped a local delivery man unloading stuff that had just been bought by my mother. The man and I lifted up a jute sack of raw rice together. The weight was no joke, so I felt like someone pushing out a shit. And my breathing turned into panting. I was still panting for a while after the rice had been set down on the porch of the shop. Plopped down on the bench to catch my breath, I found myself thinking of the panting of the water buffalos that passed in front of the shop. I thought, the weight of the rice that I lifted together with someone else was surely just as intense as the weight of the loads of those carts. Maybe the carts were even heavier. If I seemed like I was pushing a shit, but it never came out, well those water buffalos pushed their shit all the way out. It just makes sense that the cartloads that were already so heavy would multiply on the uphill incline. Little by little, as I caught my breath, my irritation at the buffalos shitting in front of the shop faded away. The opposite feeling emerged: I pitied them when I imaged how long the uphill was and how far they had already come.

Each caravan that came and went, shitting and pissing in front of my father's shop, I felt the suffering of those beasts more and more. They didn't lift their heads at all, so their snouts would almost touch the pavement of the street that was broken all to pieces. Their breathing was practically snorting, climbing the long uphill. And when they stopped smack in front of the shop, I saw their eyes where the veins looked about to burst. And their eyes were wild, as though they were trying to find a way to lift their wooden yokes that were pressuring their shoulders. If a water buffalo stood up straight for too long after the shit plopped, the cartman would snap the hard, coarse reins on the beast's nose. Maybe because of the pain on its nose, it would continue the journey pulling the cart with its bursting load.

"Why not let the water buffalo stop a while longer, so that it could gather its strength again to make it through the uphill, which still had a ways?" my heart asked. Or sometimes my heart would question why the cartmen did not relieve a little bit of the burden of stuff. "Because they're greedy," my heart would call out in exasperation.

If I saw a young woman sitting dangled in front of the tailboard of the cart, behind a curtain of tacky colored cloth, and a smile crossed her lips that were red from betel nut, while stealing a glance at me with her seductive eyes, it no longer elicited any joy in my heart. I was more interested in the eyes of the water buffalos, all red with their popping veins, looking wild, their heaving snouts panting with thick froth streaming from their mouths. My heart would catch every time I saw those passing water buffalos. And in my imagination, if there wasn't any refuse of former food spewing from their rectums, it would surely be their own intestines spewing out as they pulled the overloaded carts up that long uphill.

I thought I was becoming abnormal as I watched the agony of those beasts.

I could no longer avoid watching them go past. However, if I had other things to do and I couldn't help my father as usual, it felt like there was something missing from my life, because I no longer saw those beasts with all their suffering. It was as though there was some spiritual contact between me and them. And it even felt like I could read their thoughts, if they had thoughts, through their eyes that were staring at me.

One time at dusk when a caravan was passing again in front of my father's shop, just as I was doing my routine kind of work to help my father, it was as though I heard the water buffalos speaking. It wasn't clear what they were saying. But over time as they passed, what they were saying became clearer and clearer. It was a question. The same question directed to the same place. But the question was never answered. The question could always be heard after the water buffalo flung its shit in front of me. "Hey cart, is the uphill much longer?"

There really was no answer. Because they were asking an inanimate object that had been built and put together following a set pattern. Yes, there was always no answer. And the question would echo back forever without getting an answer.

It was always the same question directed to the same place, and it always had no answer.

Actually, I could answer it. But could they understand my language? Of course they couldn't, but that question kept getting asked of the carts after they shat in front of me, making me exasperated with the carts. "Answer them," I would say. But the carts never wanted to give an answer.

Because it was every caravan that passed, and the same chain of events kept happening, and I always urged the carts to answer (although I did this with a growl), it so happened that eventually I did hear the carts' voices. But the carts also asked, "Hey cartload, the water buffalo is asking: Is the uphill much longer?"

Of course, the cartloads couldn't answer, because they weren't the cart and also weren't the water buffalo. But the cartloads being mute made me all upset at the cartloads, too. So I started hollering at them, because every single cartload on every single cart was always mute, "Answer them," I would growl back.

Because this kept happening, each time they passed I would growl at the cartloads, each water buffalo would ask the carts and the carts would ask the cartloads, I then heard the cartloads ask the cartmen: "Hey cartmen, the water buffalo is asking: Is the uphill much longer?"

But it was like the cartmen who were sitting dangled on the front of the cart were deaf. They didn't care a lick. The caravans would go past. The questions would keep going past. Even the days went past. And the cartmen never once answered. And it got my dander up. So I growled: "Answer them."

I did this over and over, every time they passed, each iteration of the question that was put forward. And I always growled, too. In the end, because the water buffalos were nosy enough to ask the carts, and the carts were nosy enough to forward it on to the cartloads, and the cartloads were also nosy enough to pass it on to the cartmen, and I kept on growling over and over pushing the cartmen to answer, eventually I heard the cartmen say: "Shush. You're so nosy. You're just sitting there on top not doing anything. It ain't you that's put out, is it?"

I was angry to hear that answer. But the cartloads were so idiotic, just as idiotic as the carts. Because what the cartmen said to them they delivered on word for word. And when that answer reached the water buffalo, the water buffalos looked out with a gleam in their eyes that was hard for me to read.

This was the time of the revolution, the time of the War of Independence, where I was also involved. So, there was no alternative in my mind, only an uprising could possibly conquer this anguish. To see a water buffalo put to that much anguish, I shouted out angrily: "If you're human, rise up!"

But the water buffalo kept on going after its ass got beaten with a whip. That's when the humanity in me became aware that my shout had been all wrong. Because a water buffalo is not human, but a water buffalo. I should have shouted: "If you're a water buffalo, rise up!"

On another day, the same thing happened again. But it was even worse. The cart's load was so heavy that water buffalo really could not drag it up the long uphill in front of my father's shop. Two cartmen were helping to rotate the wheels by pushing its spokes. Another cartman was sitting on the wooden trace sticking out to the water buffalo's neck to keep the thing balanced.

It was to the point where the water buffalo's head was so downcast and its mouth was almost touching the pavement. The foam from its mouth was trailing out. And its groans were pulling at my heartstrings. Meanwhile its owner kept whipping its ass over and over again, fierce as anything.

If the cartman had any feeling of humanity at all, a tiny bit would have been enough, he wouldn't have had to torture the creature like that. He would pull down the drum of coconut oil hanging off the tailboard and everything would have been fine. But he preferred to torture the dumb beast rather than put himself out removing the drum full of coconut oil.

And the grunts coming out of the water buffalo's snout were pulling at my heartstrings, even now stabbing my heart. I could not think of anything else. So I cried out as loud as I could and with all the breath in my body. "Rise uuuuuuuuup."

The whole thing happened so fast. My eyes couldn't catch the whole thing perfectly. The water buffalo was freed from the harness around its neck. The cart rolled backwards. The cartload spilled everywhere. And the drum full of coconut oil lashed onto the tailboard was freed from its cords and started rolling towards the other water buffalos behind it. And the water buffalos were spooked and started bucking like horses. The woven rattan around their necks was released. And those water buffalos started running, scattering in the direction of the first water buffalo that ran off. And the whole chain of events happened to every cart on the whole hill. Until the entire road the length of the hill was full of stuff spilled everywhere and carts tipped backwards. There was even a young, newlywed wife, her lips red from betel nut, as red as her nails covered in henna, screaming to high heaven in the belly of a cart rolling backwards.

But her husband, who the night before had caressed her so passionately in the back of the cart as it went along, had run off chasing after his water buffalo that had risen up. Maybe in the thinking of that cartman, catching a water buffalo in an uprising was a better bet to guarantee his livelihood. On the other hand, the young wife who was in the midst of a disaster, it would be easy to find a replacement for her.

The Cats

If the steering committee had been smart, then it certainly would not have had Banda present a paper in the session after lunch. Banda's monotonous voice was like that of a bee buzzing around in a cramped room. What's more, his topic was out of date and involved an exhaustive commentary, quoting various officials' speeches and a range of laws, complete with number and year of promulgation. Consequently, of course, many of the participants were dozing off. Then, to overcome the drowsiness, people often left the room, whether to wash their face, take a leak, or find a friend to chat to. I was nodding off as well. Although I'd already gone out and drenched my face with water, the drowsiness struck again as soon as I sat back down in my chair. As a result of this unbearable drowsiness I was grumbling constantly about the steering committee. I complained to the friend beside me, saying that bureaucrats like Banda should not be invited to take part in the seminar just for politeness' sake because their office funded the seminar.

To overcome the drowsiness, I flicked back and forth in my notebook. I was struck by what Professor Alatas, the expert on corruption, had said. In my notes I had written down:

"The relationship between rats and development. The 1963 census in Indonesia stated that 30% of the rice crop was lost, eaten by rats. That quantity was enough to feed the population of Singapore for sixteen years. If the government wants to gain maximal results from development, a program is needed to work towards eradicating rats. In allowing rats to go unchecked, over time the animals will also influence the people's character. So there is a need to eradicate the rats, so that people won't have rats fighting against them."

Suddenly my friend tapped me on the shoulder, saying "Look at Mr. Mangku. What is he noting down so attentively?"

"Maybe it's to try and fight the drowsiness," I said. "It's more polite than chatting."

Then my attention focused on Mr. Mangku. Between the lethargy and my efforts to fight it, I remembered the time when he was governor, coming and going, occupying the grand building known as the governor's mansion. The very place where I was attending this meeting. The governor's mansion had, since the beginning, been meant for the governor to reside in. When the position of governor was moved to another city, it became the home of the district officer. After Indonesia gained independence, and the position of governor was reinstituted, the building became the governor's mansion once again.

However, during the Japanese period, it had been occupied by a Japanese military commander. From that time onward, rats began to infest the place. Various ways of exterminating them had been tried since the Japanese had left. For example, they tried traps and spreading poison. But, so the story went, it was keeping cats that was most effective in wiping out the rats.

The first attempt at extermination was installing traps. However, the results were minimal. It seemed that after one was caught, the other rats wouldn't get caught in a trap again. So, poison was put out all around the place. However the poison caused a new problem. The rats that had eaten the poison met their end in various places. Indeed, there were some that died in the governor's office or even his bedroom. Over time, a foul smell spread through the whole of the governor's mansion. At first the bad smell was really annoying, but then the inhabitants' noses became immune. An immunized sense of smell seemed to spread to all the staff of the governor's office, particularly those that often appeared before him. Even the noses of people who only came now and then became immune, since not a single one pinched their nose in the governor's mansion.

When there was a change of governor, the new governor immediately smelt the spreading putrefaction. His first action was to get rid of the rottenness completely. This was done in many ways. All the buildings were cleaned and rinsed with carbolic acid. The equipment was replaced. And from time to time an air freshener was sprayed around. Especially when a visitor from the central government came. All to disguise the putrid smell.

"However you try to cover it up, something that's rotten will always smell awful, Governor," said the minister, when he was about to leave for Jakarta after staying overnight in the governor's mansion.

So the governor called his staff to discuss the rotten smell that just would not go away. But no one could think of a way because, their thinking went, it couldn't have been caused by the dead rats. The governor's mansion had long since been cleaned. If one of the dead rats had been missed when this was done, it would surely have already dried out and would no longer smell. However, the minister had spoken.

So Professor Alatas was invited to help solve the problem. And although the professor was an expert in the field of corruption, as soon as he arrived in the governor's mansion, he knew what had afflicted it.

"There are too many rats in the mansion, Mr. Governor. It's best to eradicate them in a natural way. You should keep cats," said the professor while stroking his thick, black beard. "Using traps is not effective. If one trap succeeds, other rats will avoid it, even if it has a very enticing bait. Rats have an amazingly high IQ, Mr. Governor."

So, they acquired five cats: one male and four females. No one knew the reason for this gender split. The professor never gave one. Perhaps a psychologist or sociologist could give an answer.

Anyhow, the cats were very fertile, even if the rats were even more so. The coming of the cats, who became more numerous as time went on, really did send the rats running helter-skelter. They moved to other buildings nearby. The governor's mansion was now truly free of rats. The smell of rat urine, that had irritated guests' noses, now disappeared. They no longer needed to spray air freshener when guests were visiting.

Looking after the cats required a special budget. Not just for their food, but also to pay for specialist staff, besides a vet that would oversee their health. But the main thing was that cats can catch rabies. The lives of the governor and other high-ranking staff could be at risk. The government could be undermined, couldn't it? Indeed the cost mounted. But fortunately it did not need the approval of the regional assembly, as long as the money could be found from another legitimate budget. What's more, it would be no joke if the budget for looking after cats was discussed by members of the regional assembly, which was generally very critical.

The cats' presence was very effective, even though all these cats never caught a single rat, since they'd scampered away to nearby houses or safe places. Yet in truth, the cats never put much effort into their duty, that is, getting rid of the rats. Since they were well looked after and were fed nutritious food, the population multiplied from month to month. And they also grew to be fat. Their steps became plodding. They curled up and relaxed on all the guest chairs. They even slept on the chairs. If there were guests, it was hard to chase the cats away. The only way to shift them was to carry them.

The time came to cut back the number of cats to the number needed to prevent rats sneaking in. However, the governor had grown used to having lots of cats. And the behavior of the little kittens was a pleasant entertainment, especially for the governor himself. They, the cats, had become inseparable from the governor's mansion.

Cats are among the animals with the lowest IQs. Definitely lower than rats. And the way the governor spoiled them sometimes made them rude to the governor's own guests. Besides not wanting to shift from the chairs that were meant to be for guests, sometimes they would even, without a second thought, pee on a guest's trousers or jump up onto the lap of ladies who were in the middle of listening to a speech. Yet no one was put off coming to the governor's mansion.

But when an ambassador from a neighboring country came to visit the governor, the cats' behavior caused an uproar. The governor's wife seemed to become hysterical. Her face was red while the guests were there and turned apoplectic when they had left. The thing was, an incident had occurred as a result of the cats' behavior. They were all caterwauling in a heat the whole night, to the point that the ambassador and his wife couldn't sleep.

"Get rid of all those cats!" the governor's wife shouted after the guests had left. But the issue wasn't as simple as shouting. Because the cats had done a service by protecting the governor's mansion against rats.

A businessman who had made his money cutting down the forest on an island, to the point that the whole island appeared yellow if viewed from the air, also heard about the incident. He came, bringing a cat in a cardboard box.

"There are already too many cats here," said the governor's wife, rather acidly, in a tone quite different from the one that she would normally use with this guest.

"But this cat is not a native cat, madam. Native cats do indeed cause trouble. There are more and more of them and the only work they do is to sleep. They're unattractive, too. This cat is a Persian cat, madam, but I brought it from Hong Kong. Before I went to Hong Kong, I already had a male one. I brought it from Paris. But when I came back from Hong Kong recently, I found out that the cat from Paris had died. It was run over by a car, madam. So I brought this one. Sometime when I am abroad again, I'll look for a partner for it. So you can have a pair. Multinational cats."

The governor's wife was mesmerized looking at the cat with its thick fur and piercingly beautiful eyes. After stroking its fur while it sat on her lap, the governor's wife said, "How can it mix with the other cats here?"

The businessman, who didn't know the history of the cats in the governor's mansion, answered curtly: "Get rid of them all, madam."

But the governor's wife could not bear to get rid of all the cats from the mansion. The governor couldn't bear to either. He said, "Although I can eradicate the thieves in my office, it just seems inhumane to eradicate the cats here."

"Ah, that will be taken care of, Mr. Governor," said the businessman.

And when the governor and his wife returned from overseas, fulfilling an invitation from the ambassador who had once been their guest, they found their home very quiet. Something felt missing. For a long time, the governor was in a daze, thinking about what had happened during his absence. Then, when a pair of Persian cats came meowing out from his children's' bedroom, he knew that the dozens of cats, the creatures that had become inseparable from the setting of the governor's mansion, had gone.

And the governor did not ask anyone how the cats disappeared. In truth, in his heart of hearts he was grateful. Because when he'd been in Rome, he had seen lots of cats in the Colosseum, that ancient, partly ruined edifice. He'd had a feeling of horror when he saw those cats residing beneath gloomy recesses in the twilight.

Apparently, the cats of the governor's mansion had been put in a truck, then cast out in the middle of a distant jungle. A jungle that had not yet been cleared by that businessman. And when the cats, in a manner similar to regular people, who had all this time been spoiled, were suddenly thrown into the wild jungle, many of them met their fate. But those that were strong lived wild, in accordance with the existing laws of the jungle. And at some point, those that were still alive found their way home. They found the governor having an afternoon nap besides his wife.

"Governor, what did we do wrong, to get cast out? Was it because we are only a native breed? Although we had already done you the service of getting rid of the rats?" they asked, as if making a threat.

The governor was woken by his wife shaking him. His wife had herself been woken by the shouts of her husband. Over and over the governor prayed for forgiveness, but every time he slept he dreamt of the protesting cats, to the point he was afraid to sleep. The pills the doctor gave him so that he could sleep soundly did not help, because the dreams always came when he slept. Seeing the physical condition of the governor deteriorating, the doctors in the hospital held a kind of seminar about the diagnosis and treatment for the sickness that afflicted the governor, if what he was suffering from was really a sickness.

This seminar, which showed the doctors' expertise and intelligence, went on for quite a long time. Days even. It must be understood that as soon as they got into the seminar again, there was always a doctor that would be called away to their ward for a patient emergency.

And when the seminar finished, the decision was that the governor had to be sent to a hospital abroad. It was to be noted that the local doctors were not lacking in expertise, but the medical equipment was inadequate, and what they had was already outdated.

Yet, when the decision was delivered, the governor had already left on the advice of a spiritual advisor to visit an elder who was known for his supernatural powers and had patients from almost all over the modern world.

However, the government did not wait for the governor to recover from his illness. An acting governor was appointed. But by that time, rats had already started making their home in the governor's mansion again.

And when I raised my head, Mr. Mangku was still writing in his notebook, although more often he was massaging the bridge of his nose. Meanwhile, there remained just a few seminar participants still sitting in their places, out of politeness to Banda, who kept reading his article from the lectern.

My drowsiness began to strike again.

The Old Order

J ust at dawn when the rays of the sun began to peek over the
hilltops to the east of the lake, the sound of a gong could be
heard drilling into the ears of the residents, even those who
lived far away on the side of the hill. This gong announced a decree
from the village head.

"Can't be a gong for collective labor, because this is Friday,"
thought Leman as he weeded his field of chili peppers.

Almost every day since the villages around the lake had been
freed from the troops of the PRRI regional rebellion, the residents
were roped in for collective labor. If it wasn't fixing the roads, it
was cutting down the banana trees around the outskirts of the
village, because banana trees could be used as cover by the PRRI
troops if they attacked the village. If it wasn't cleaning up the yard
in front of the sub-district head's office, it was bound to be making
a bamboo fence along the whole length of the road so the PRRI
troops couldn't break through unimpeded into the village. Only
every Friday they didn't have collective labor, because the window
of time on that day was so short, leading up to congregational
Friday prayers.

Because of this, Leman felt relieved. Even though there was the
beat of the gong, it certainly wouldn't bother his plans for that day,
because he was intending to go to the sub-district offices to ask for
a marriage license for Ramalah, his first-born daughter. Without a
license from the Sub-District Religious Affairs Office, no officiant
could marry off Ramalah. But the marriage had to be executed

immediately. If not, it would become terribly late. The man who was to become Ramalah's husband would have the opportunity to come up with more excuses. That could not happen. If that happened, ugh, ugh, ugh. Leman couldn't think about it for too long.

Ramalah was already three months pregnant. The whole while the man refused to marry her. The pretext was that she was not a virgin before she got with him. But Ramalah insisted that this very man was the only one who had ever taken her to bed. Only after some coaxing and a promise to buy him a bicycle was the man ready to marry Ramalah. Even so, the man set yet another condition. He only wanted to marry her; he would not come home to live with her.

"Fine. The important thing is that Ramalah gets married, even if later on she'll be alone for the rest of her life. The problem is the child in Ramalah's belly needs to have a legitimate father," Leman told himself in his heart when the man put forward that extra condition. The decision had just been reached the night before. And if they didn't go through with the marriage today, maybe the man would renege again.

When the sun had risen over the hilltops, Leman was already trudging along the main road to the sub-district offices. From the coffee shop at the village intersection, someone hollered at him not to go to the sub-district that day, because there was going to be a raid. But Leman didn't care. He was not afraid to be caught up in a raid. He knew that he had all the identity papers he needed.

The main road was so empty. It wasn't like a normal Friday, which was the market day in Chalk Village. But that wasn't what Leman was thinking about. His thoughts were focused on the problem of Ramalah's marriage. According to the religious scholars that Leman followed, the obligation to marry off a girl fell to her father. The officiant just acted as a witness. If it was that simple to marry someone off according to their religion, there was actually no need to go to the Religious Affairs Office to get a license. If the government needed a record, that could be arranged later. But a marriage like that did not follow the regulations. So now suddenly Leman felt that the regulations were made just to make life more difficult.

Difficult or not, he had to go to the Religious Affairs Office that very day. And because he was so convinced of this, he almost ruined a huge plan that was going to become a national point of pride.

Because ...

The president had decreed that on the upcoming Independence Day, the Republic of Indonesia had to be proclaimed a country free of illiteracy. Because of this, there had to be raids to find out if the Indonesian nation really was free of illiteracy after all this time campaigning to combat it. For our province, the governor had ordered that the raid be done in Chalk Village, his home village. He did this for its symbolism, because as a favored son of the nation, the governor had to show the president that his home village had dutifully followed the president's instructions. And the governor himself would come with the committee to oversee the raid.

"Do not embarrass me," the governor instructed the district head a few days prior.

And the district head passed on the message to the sub-district head, "Do not make the governor angry at me."

And the sub-district head ordered the village heads next to the lake, "If there are still illiterate people, I will throw the village head in jail."

And the village head ordered the village patrol, "Sound the gong. Tell everyone who is illiterate to head up into the jungle."

But Leman only heard the sound of the gong. He didn't hear the strident cries of the village patrol. So it happened that Leman was suddenly intercepted at the edge of Chalk Village by one of the officials conducting the raid. He was taken to in front of a chalkboard that was leaning up against some chairs by the side of the main road. All eyes were on him, staring him down.

"Read," instructed one of the officials as he slapped his pointer against the white letters on the board.

"Oh God, what disaster will befall Ramalah?" he screamed in his head as his eyes darted left and right, looking for a way to escape.

The official repeated his order over and over to the point of barking, and there was no way for Leman to escape. His whole body was bathed in sweat, not just because of putting himself out by walking all the way from his house that morning, but also because he was trying to hide his fear.

He was tongue-tied. Not only because he was afraid of the barking, but also because he actually couldn't read the letters that the official was pointing to. For a second he remembered his God, and he wanted to recite a prayer so that he might receive a miracle. But he didn't know what prayer he should recite at that moment.

The face of the governor, which was usually so tan, fell ashen as his anger boiled up when Leman was herded toward the officials overseeing the raid. He rebuked the district head mercilessly. The district head felt the rebuke, and passed it right on to his sub-district head. And the sub-district head passed it on by barking at the village head. The village head had only a brief moment to think fast, as fast as a fighter jet flying over the village when they were searching for the remnants of PRRI troops. He knew the governor must be feeling very embarrassed, because there was still illiteracy, and in his very own village to boot. So he immediately responded to the barking of the sub-district head with a calm tone of voice.

"But Mr. Governor, this man is not from our village here."

The governor's face suddenly lit up. Then he said to the Head of the Raid Team who had come all the way from Jakarta for this: "See, it's true, what I said. Not one person in my home village is illiterate."

"So where is he from?" asked the Head of the Raid Team.

"From Hillside Village, sir," said the village head quickly.

"Now don't put me in a corner, eh?" the district head suddenly piped up in opposition to the village head's answer.

Once again the village head showed his smarts. "Actually, he does live in Hillside Village, sir. But he originally was a resident of Grindstone Village."

"Yes, that's the correct explanation. Because last Sunday I had a raid in Hillside Village. There was no one in Hillside Village who is still illiterate," said the district head proudly, because Hillside Village was the village where his parents had been born.

"We believe you," said one of the people from Jakarta calmly. "The trouble is, how should we put it in the report I will write for the president?"

This was a question that was not easy to answer. Even if Leman was not a resident of Chalk Village, and wasn't a resident of Hillside Village either, wasn't he still a resident of the province under this particular governor? All the people in attendance started to whisper to the people standing next to them. And the sub-district head stepped close to Leman. Then he whispered in Leman's ear. "Damn you," he said.

After rounds and rounds of negotiations, the bureaucrats that gathered there finally proved once again the wonder of consultation and consensus. Thus, the Head of the Raid Team from Jakarta said to the many journalists in attendance, "The UN must learn from Indonesia how to combat illiteracy."

And the governor added, "We have carried out the instructions of the president perfectly."

But not for Leman ...

Because the short consultation by the bureaucrats that came along for the raid had decided that the illiteracy still found in Leman had to be combatted immediately. That task was given to the sub-district head, who would be overseen by the district head.

And the sub-district head assured them that in the span of three months Leman would no longer be illiterate. In this way on the upcoming Independence Day, the president could announce to the whole world that Indonesia was free of illiteracy. Then the delegation from the capital left Chalk Village with their faces beaming.

But Leman was left behind dejected, all the more dejected by the barking and insults of the sub-districts employees. He almost fainted when the sub-district head gave him a punishment of carrying forty sacks of cement to the floodgate that they were building at the foot of Mulch Hill, because the floodgate was located two hours away along a path on the embankments of paddy fields and no vehicle could get there. And he couldn't carry these sacks himself, either. He would have to pay someone else. And if he paid them, that meant he couldn't buy the bike for Ramalah's future husband.

Crying, Leman pled his case with the village head. He explained all the difficulties he was going through. But the village head could only advise him to meet with the sub-district head. With a flash of hope, Leman met with the sub-district head.

"You've made my life difficult, Leman. Made life difficult for the district head. Made life difficult for the governor. You've even made life difficult for the president. You know what? I'm adding ten more sacks of cement that you have to carry over there," said the sub-district head before Leman could even finish the story of his difficulties.

Leman should have met with the district head to ask for mercy. But his experience with the sub-district head had taught him a lesson. That was: the higher you take the case, the higher the cost of settling it.

There was no other way for him now. He had to surrender Ramalah to her fate.

And when the president announced that Indonesia was free of illiteracy on Independence Day as had been the original plan, a baby who had just come out from his mother's womb cried. The birth was two months early. But Leman felt ten years older when he thought about the question the baby would soon be asking, "Who is my daddy?"

Third-Class Passenger

Dali met an old friend on the ship *Kerenci*, sailing from Padang to Jakarta, as a third-class passenger. They met after they had been at sea for a night, when they were lining up for the head. They had already seen each other in their bunks where they laid alongside other people, but at that point they paid no attention to each other, much less struck up a conversation. They only noticed each other when they were in line waiting to clean up for the start of the day. At first they looked at each other, then looked away. They looked at each other again and looked away again. When they looked at each other a third time, they didn't look away. They both smiled.

"You're Dali, aren't you?" said the one.

"Are you Nuan?" said Dali, answering with a question.

They embraced, with their arms still holding all their toiletries, soap, toothbrushes and towels.

"I haven't seen you in such a long time."

"It really has been a long time."

They asked and answered each other's questions. Intently. In the time it took for a few people to go in and out of the head, they were still asking and answering. Amid all that, Dali's thoughts wandered back to the distant past.

Nuan had a twin brother; Nain was his name. You could tell who was who, because one wasn't as stout as the other. They always went everywhere together. Folks say that twins often have the same tastes, including in women. Folks say that this only becomes apparent later on, namely when they come into competition to win a girl's heart. The kind of man who was idolized in the early revolution, especially who was idolized by the girls, was a soldier with a samurai sword tied on his waist and military boots strapped on his feet. Nuan and Nain only achieved the rank of sergeant first class with the duty of basic training for new soldiers in the state army. Because of their low rank, they did not have the right to wear those heady symbols of officers. Both of them also felt they were not getting the attention of Wati, the girl next door. And when the commander of the Hizbullah Islamic militia, Colonel Hasan, invited him to join with the rank of second lieutenant, Nuan left his duties in the state army. So he could get the same rank, Nain went off to join the Communist-aligned Indonesian Red Army militia.

"What does a difference in militia matter? The important thing is to both be lieutenants, both get samurai swords and wear military boots," they said, figuring that Wati would begin to notice them.

∝

The longer they had been in militias with different ideologies, the more there grew a silent enmity within each of their hearts, as there emerged a competition to win Wati's heart. But neither of them was bold enough to cast a net to catch her. Nuan always talked about the holy war if he stopped by Wati's house. Meanwhile, Nain spoke of the people's revolution. They once debated in front of Wati to defend their respective goals in the struggle. But usually they would go one at a time because they really didn't have leave at the same time. Of course, on those occasions they would talk up their own militias.

It was Nuan who was able to win over Wati in the end. It happened after the government implemented its rationalization policy, consolidating all armed units into the Indonesian National

Army. With that policy, the rank of all officers merged from outside the Indonesian National Army was lowered by two levels. Nuan got a new position as staff in the logistical section, while Nain was in the fighting units on the front. Both still equally talked up their new posts to Wati, even though they no longer had the right to carry a samurai sword or wear military boots.

Wati's father had a practical take on deciding who would be a match for his daughter. He said, "An officer in the logistical section can better provide for the needs of your household, while an officer at the front means a higher likelihood that you'll soon be a widow."

"Even though you always return my kisses, Nuan is the one who you'll make your husband," Nain reproached Wati.

"What can I do, if my father wants Nuan?" answered Wati pitifully.

Nain was already training for radical action, both because he had joined the Red Army and because he had been at the front for a long time, and he held Wati close to him. And they ground up against each other with their breasts flush with excitement. And when they were about to cross over the boundary line, Wati realized she was going to be Nuan's wife. The grinding calmed down. From then on, they never saw each other again, because Nain's unit was always moving from place to place, from one island to another, each stricken with military crises because the officers were not satisfied with the political policies on military affairs after the revolution.

 C8

When a military crisis broke out in the form of the PRRI rebellion back in West Sumatra, once again Nain's unit was tasked with stamping it out. On the other side, Nuan joined with the PRRI rebels staking out positions in the jungle. But Wati remained in the city. When Nain came back and ran across Wati, who at that point already had two children, the fire in both their breasts reignited. They ground against each other again. And again. And again. The fire in Nain's chest mixed with vengeance, a potent mixture of forbidden love and ideological enmity with his brother. For Wati, although she lusted after him, she only went through with it after consideration: rather than service some other soldier drunk with victory, it was better to receive Nain, who would at the same time serve as her protector. She suppressed any thoughts and feelings of morality far down in the depths of her heart. If she held herself back from screaming, then she was able to stifle the cries just because of the necessity to make peace with the situation.

Finally, after the rebellion lost, Nuan went back to join the Indonesian National Army with a rank that was again reduced by two levels, down to a sergeant. He came face-to-face with Nain who was already a captain who had won victory in battle, and this in front of Wati. For a moment—just a single moment—they stood looking at each other as though entranced, then they embraced as twin brothers. Not a single word was uttered. And Wati ran to the back room and then to the house next door. She ran from the situation that would be unbearable if it blew up. She didn't emerge again until the two men had gone.

ⓒ♋

At first it was a feeling, then a suspicion, and eventually he was sure that something had happened between Wati and Nain. His heart was wounded, then he was angry and then came a hatred that gave birth to an unquenchable vengeance. But he was a soldier whose side had lost. A man who was now a sergeant after his rank kept getting lowered. And over there was Nain, who had become a captain because his side won. Because of his victory he had slept with Wati, the wife of his own twin brother.

"Betrayal. The whole thing's a betrayal," he kept shouting. But he was a soldier whose side had lost. What could the loser in battle really do? For Nuan there was nothing besides lose and then accept it without being able to do anything, or even think anything. With those feelings he took back Wati, who brought their two children. "That Wati is a woman who has been beaten by history," he said to pacify the side of his heart that was flaring up.

All of a sudden, the script of history was flipped. The communist rebellion broke out. Nain, who was a captain and just promoted to major, went with the communists. Now it was he who was defeated. He was captured and thrown in jail. Every ounce of Nuan's heart cried out. "You feel it now." But Nain was his twin brother, born of the same mother's womb. They began their ideological split because they hitched rides on the different trains that history had prepared for them. Did he have to wreak vengeance for Wati sleeping with Nain by going himself and sleeping with Inna, Nain's wife, who was beautiful and young, and who was now staying in his home?

No. He couldn't do it. Inna was the wife of his twin brother. Why would he have to wreak vengeance on his own twin brother who was at that moment being tortured for his ideology? But when he remembered how Wati had betrayed him, the wounds in his heart tore open afresh. He left Wati who was lying by his side. He went to Inna's room with a burning, consuming lust for vengeance against Wati.

However Nuan only stood dazed, looking at Inna take off her clothes as she sobbed. Then he went out of the house slamming the door and walked along the edge of the main road, which was dark because the electricity had long been cut off from the main generator, which was old and broken.

 C3

"It's been a real long time, yeah, since we met?" said one of them after they wandered aimlessly together to the railing at the bow of the ship and looked at the heaving of the open ocean.

"Yeah, it's been a real long time."

"All of a sudden we've become old."

"All the same, we cannot forget everything."

"Truly."

Marah, Who Endured

Because he was descended from an aristocratic family in Padang, after he married he received the hereditary title Marah, like his father before him. So his full name became Marah Ahmad. Due to his ancestry, his education and social connections, as well as his position as a senior native official in the Town Hall, he was part of a respected elite.

Once he realized that Holland would lose the war with Japan, he was beset with anxiety. Intense anxiety. From what he had read he knew that the Japanese empire was dominated by a fascist military with its totalitarian rule, meaning that their power was untouchable. Meaning that the law of the land did not apply to them. Meaning that they were allowed to do anything they liked to the people. Marah Ahmad was not mentally prepared to face the impending change.

As a civil servant who had for years served a legal system based on the prevailing laws, he was nervous facing this fascist military government. He did not know whether he would be approved to continue working by the Japanese or not. If not, well, so what? That would be for the best. If he was required to continue working, would he be able? He was certain he wouldn't.

However, his feelings were rent asunder by the events following the arrival of the Japanese military. Initially he was surprised. Indeed, he almost could not believe that this army of short men wearing clothes the color of ocher, the same color as the dirt, and were disheveled and untidy, could defeat the Dutch military with its magnificently turned out officers. He was reminded of what Chatib Jarin had said, "These Japanese are like monkeys, how come they were able to defeat the Dutch without a war? And how were the Dutch able to colonize us for hundreds of years?"

Although he was sorry for the loss of his Dutch superiors, he understood when all the people welcomed the Japanese, who were viewed as liberators and promising a new life. Perhaps because the people had never felt themselves friends with the Dutch rulers. There was a gulf between them. Indeed, even Marah Ahmad himself felt there was a distance between himself as an official and the Dutch, even though it was stupid. His relations with the Dutch were only in the office; outside of it the bridge connecting them collapsed.

The military commander of these liberators requested that the community's leaders maintain the order and safety of all cities and villages. And these leaders said to the people, "Let's show these Japanese that we can manage the affairs of our own country without them." So the situation was indeed peaceful—during both day and night. The Japanese military were not really needed. The people treated the Japanese soldiers and officers they met on the road as ordinary foreign guests. It was only little children that liked to shout "Banzai Nippon" if they passed by.

However, after two weeks of peaceful conditions, a commotion broke out in the Chinese quarter. When the news reached Marah Ahmad's ears, he thought that the war between the Chinese and Japanese in China had spread to the city of Padang. But when he realized that it was the local people looting Chinese shops, Marah Ahmad cursed. "Up until now it has been peaceful. How come suddenly there is looting? Where is the People's Security Committee? Why have our people suddenly become barbaric?"

"What have the Chinese done wrong? Oh, is it because Japan is at war with them? What is the connection?" he grumbled to Chatib Jarin when they met again.

"Because the Chinese are infidels, sir," said Chatib Jarin.

"At the time of the Prophet Muhammad, Muslims treated unbelievers well, Chatib."

"The infidels there were Arabs, like the Muslims. Here they are Chinese. They are not the same as us, sir."

"Ah, a lousy excuse," muttered Marah Ahmad.

ᘓ

The following day more Chinese shops were looted. Even the inhabitants of the villages at the edge of the city came. Marah Ahmad could see it from his office window. People passed from the left empty handed. Those coming from the right were carrying away all sorts of items. There were some carrying rolls of cloth over their shoulders. There were those who carried off cutlery, kitchenware and household goods. Some carried bicycle tires or spare parts. Even children joined in, sometimes looting things they did not even know how to use.

"Barbaric. It's barbaric, all of it," said Marah Ahmad with a voice that resounded through all the rooms in the office, to the point that the workers, who had gathered at the office door to watch the people who had been looting, turned towards him.

"Hey, Kimin. How have our people come to this? Where is our noble religion? Where are our exalted customs?" he said to a nearby colleague.

"I don't know, sir," said his colleague. Then he continued, "Someone said it was the Japanese that started it, sir."

"They were also looting?"

"Someone said, some of our people are Japanese agents. On their right arm they had a cloth band bearing the letter F. They were accompanied by two soldiers. It was them that broke down the shop door. Then they threw the things outside. Then they told the people to start looting. The soldiers just watched, sir. A row of Chinese shops on that road were looted. Then the people went to another road. Chinese shops were ordered robbed there as well, sir," said Kimin.

"Previously they asked people to maintain the peace. It was so peaceful. But now they tell people to cause disorder. What kind of government is this? A government of pirates?" said Marah Ahmad, his emotions boiling over. Then he went into his office. He sat limply on a chair. For a long time he sat there. After that he rested his head on the chair's back rest. As he looked at the ceiling he thought, and thought hard. But he could not accept even one of the reasons for the looting.

Suddenly, sometime past midday, there was an uproar from the direction of the main road. In unison the Town Hall officials bounded towards the door. Marah Ahmad stopped thinking. Listless as he was, he followed them to the door. "What's happening?" he asked.

From an official who had just come from outside the office, Marah Ahmad got the story that the Japanese Military Police had suddenly arrived. Then they shot two looters. Sluggishly, Marah Ahmad returned to his chair. He sat stunned. Slowly a picture of events emerged in his mind. Initially the Japanese had requested the people maintain the peace. Then they told the people to loot. Then the next day they shot the looters. Those were the facts. But why?

This question kept on repeating itself in his mind. It was stopped by the appearance of a Japanese officer, dressed neatly with a white collar emerging from the neck of his jacket. He wore boots that came up almost to his knees, and a samurai sword hung from his left hip. He was accompanied by an adjutant, dressed almost as neatly. An Indonesian wearing a jacket and tie was with them, with a face Marah Ahmad could not quite place.

Marah Ahmad received his guests awkwardly, since he did not know how he should greet them. Then the officer spoke haltingly in Japanese. The tie-wearing Indonesian translated for him. Although

Marah Ahmad understood, he could not fathom the officer's real meaning. The series of words, according to Marah Ahmad's understanding, was, "Nippon-Indonesia together. However, this country is not secure. Everywhere there is disorder. The Indonesian people cannot manage their own country. Beginning today the military must govern. This officer will be the Mayor. Nippon-Indonesia together."

"You're sly," Marah Ahmad cursed in his heart, to the point that his whole body trembled in containing his anger.

Then Marah Ahmad saw a poster stuck up on the wall of the front room of the office. It contained a declaration stating that commencing today the military was to take over control of government. All the offices and shops were to open as normal. The people were forbidden to fly the Indonesian flag. On the journey home, the poster was spread across the walls and fences of people's homes.

Only now Marah Ahmad understood the drama the military had constructed. They didn't like the country being run by the people according to the people's methods. The military wanted to take control and have authority over everything in the land. Since the country could be kept peaceful by the people themselves, they provoked a situation where there was disorder. This disorder was then made a pretext for taking power into their hands. But why was the disorder directed at the Chinese?

In the following days he realized why the Chinese shops were made the target of the looting. Not because of the hostilities of the two peoples in China, but rather because it was an easy way to play on popular sentiments—sentiments that had grown and were nurtured by the colonial government all this time, so that the people remained divided by race, differences in ethnicity, and religious differences.

Marah Ahmad couldn't accept the military's tactics and methods. If they wanted to have power, why did they have to use these dirty tactics and methods? After all, the people would not dare oppose the military with its weapons.

The first day that Marah Ahmad returned to the office, he came half-heartedly. By the time he went home, his heart wasn't in it at all. What had happened was that when all the staff were gathered on the field beside the Town Hall to join the ceremony for the raising of the Japanese rising sun flag, an old official with a bloated body was struck on his head by a soldier. This was because at the time of bowing in the direction of the flag, he only bowed his head. So more willingness drained from Marah Ahmad's heart. Then when the Mayor, a soldier, called him to appear before him, he did not bow. He only bowed his head, as was normally done when facing a Dutch mayor. The Japanese started yelling. Although Marah Ahmad did not understand a word of Japanese, he could tell he was being berated. Then he was ordered out. Just as he was going through the door, he was called again. Marah Ahmad realized he was being ordered to bow. Then he bowed. Precisely at that moment the last willingness left his heart. Tomorrow he would not come to work.

According to the story his oldest child told to Dali, years later, ten days after stopping coming to work, his father was picked up by the Japanese Military Police. Fifteen days after he was arrested, he was freed due to the efforts of his cousin who had a Japanese wife. However almost his entire body was covered in bruise marks. And his big toe was bandaged because the nail had been pulled out when he was tortured during his imprisonment. The only sentence that he could say for the next few days at home was "Nippon-Indonesia together. Nippon-Indonesia together."

Shadows

Dali was not an ordinary person. He had become a public figure, indeed, a public phenomenon. His life was always cast in a bright shining light, sparkling with beautiful colors. More so than a star actor performing on stage, since the actor playing Julius Caesar, or King Lear, or Macbeth only glitters to the edge of the stage. Then when the curtain has fallen, or outside the theatre, they return to being ordinary humans. Sometimes it's like in the past when a beggar finished playing the mythical hero Gatotkaca in a village drama performance; after the show is over he goes back from hero to beggar. Whereas it was as if Dali was on the world stage, no longer bound by a country's borders. People said that Dali was this way because he never lived in the darkness, during either night or day. Meaning he always lived in a shining brightness, full of light.

So Dali was always accompanied by shadows. Many shadows. There were short ones and long ones, fat ones and thin ones. Of course, wherever he went he was always accompanied by shadows. For the shadows were his very own. As shadows do, the shadows always imitated just what Dali was doing. Whether Dali was eating or sleeping, taking a stroll, or having an affair.

Not once did the shadows part from him. And Dali was convinced the shadows existed because of him.

Without him, the shadows would disappear. Because of this, the shadows all needed him. Really needed him. This was different from other people, who never cared about their own shadows, since they liked living shady lives in the dark. As if shadows were not important creatures. "Imagine," said Dali to his own shadows when he was squatting on the toilet, "what kind of person lives without shadows, except for shady people who like being in the dark?"

Dali also let the shadows imitate exactly what he was doing. What was wrong with all the shadows imitating what he was doing? After all, they did him no harm. Yet however precise the imitation, one thing that the shadows could not get was all the pleasure that Dali imbibed. "You can imitate everything that I do, but don't imagine that you can enjoy what I taste. Since all those pleasures are not yours by right. That is axiomatic."

Dali's sparkling life in the limelight soon reached the ears of the palace. So the king called his prime minister and questioned him.

"It's true, Your Majesty," answered the prime minister, who knew where this was going.

"Kill him," ordered the king.

After thinking a while, the prime minister said, "Wouldn't you like to know what this Dali is like first?"

"Very well then, arrest him and bring him here," said the king.

"Having people killed or arrested is indeed within Your Majesty's powers. But if he is killed or arrested, he will become greater than his own fate. He will become the stuff of historical myth. A myth heady enough to get the people demonstrating. Just imagine it, Your Majesty. Demonstrations these days are truly barbaric."

"What's your point?"

"Invite him here. Embrace him. So that Your Majesty will still be greater than Dali."

"All right, invite him here. Greet him as though inviting a gladiator or a top celebrity," said the king.

Dali couldn't avoid making assumptions. He thought he would be raised to an honored position of state. Perhaps Prime Minister, or at least Coordinating Minister, as they had in Indonesia. But those jobs required more brown-nosing than big thinking. So he would reject them.

When Dali arrived at the palace, he was greeted by a row of beauties with bulging bosoms and swelling behinds, like *jaipong* dancers. The inside of the palace was bathed in sparkling light. The king's clothes were beaded and he had rows and rows of stars on the right and left of his chest, even reaching down to his pot belly. The king waited in the center of the large room. The king looked so grand and powerful to Dali. More enthralling than the kings in the historical soap operas that he had seen on television.

The lighting that shone gleaming around the room cast no shadow from the king. But the walls were lined with the kingdom's officials and their wives. Those are the king's shadows, thought Dali. Suddenly all the lights dimmed. A spotlight on the left wall shone brightly in the direction of the queen, who appeared at the end of the room. A shadow accompanied her. The king introduced Dali to the queen. Dali bowed while clasping her hands in greeting. But Dali's shadow—it was as if it tightly embraced the queen's shadow. They both fell tussling on the floor. Dali looked around. Along the wall it looked as though there were black shadows, which seemed to be watching the three people in the middle of the room. When all the lights were turned back on, Dali could not see his shadow. Nor that of the queen. Even when he went home, his shadow did not follow him. And when he turned on the light in the living room, he saw the shadow of the king's bloated body sitting reclined on the sofa.

"You're not my shadow," said Dali. "You should be with the king. What are you doing here?"

"I'm annoyed. Fed up. Upset. The king has lots of shadows. All of them are sycophants, so that I, who've been loyal since he was born, am not paid any attention anymore," said the king's shadow.

"So?"

"When I saw your shadow following the queen's shadow, so that you lost your own shadow, I thought I should follow you. Because you need a shadow. It would be really strange if a public figure like you didn't have a shadow," said the shadow.

As a major public figure, who always had ideas that were beyond the reach of most people, Dali then offered the king's shadow the chance to swap places. He would become the king's shadow and the king's shadow would become him. "You want to be the king's shadow?" asked the shadow.

"Oh, no. Not on my life would I want to be. I only want to disguise myself as you. Just for one day, OK?"

"OK."

As a shadow, Dali could freely enter the palace with its layers of security. He could also freely enter all the many rooms in the palace, with their varied designs. They were all grand, indeed spectacular. There was a room like there was in the film *Star Trek*. There was one like the garden in the film *The Last Days of Pompeii*. However, it wasn't that amazing in Dali's eyes.

While Dali was still disguised as the king's shadow he entered the Cabinet Room. The cabinet was in session, under the leadership of the prime minister. Just at that moment the prime minister was saying, "Now then, you know what kind person this Dali is. He's skinny like Nashar. Unconventional like Affandi. His eyes bulge like... like... like who, eh?" For a second he was quiet, as he was reminded of a former president, whom he thought not proper to remark on. Then he said: "Yes, he's like Picasso, if we stick to painters as examples. He has become a public figure because he is often, very often, in the press and on television. His speeches, sermons, and statements are often quoted, his poems sung in many musical and literary performances. Isn't that true?"

"He wouldn't be anything without the press and television. So he can't be compared to the king. The king would still be the king, even without media coverage," said a minister.

"All right, then ban the press and television from covering him," suggested another minister.

"Banning things is outdated. It's not fitting with the spirit of reform," the prime minister chimed in.

"If that's the case, how about balancing it out with lots of coverage of the king?" suggested yet another.

"As we all know, the king doesn't do anything worth being covered. Would it make sense to have media coverage of the king eating, or of the king sleeping?"

"Once again I warn you. Use proper and correct language when referring to the king. The king doesn't eat, but rather dines, doesn't sleep but reposes. He's not sick, but indisposed. He doesn't drink, but imbibes. He is not clothed, but... but what, eh?" said the prime minister, a little loudly.

"If that's the case, I suppose the king will never die, will he?" whispered a minister to the colleague to his left.

"Indeed, rather he'll pass away," he responded.

"For things that are sacred, or regarded as sacred, we need to use classical language, as Indonesian people do when using classical Sanskrit to name new buildings that are being consecrated," interjected the minister sitting to the right.

"So, what is the problem with Dali then?" asked a minister wearing a general's uniform with all its decorations.

"Dali is too famous. Too popular. More so than the king," answered the prime minister. "It compromises the monarchy's credibility."

"What's the king's opinion?"

"He has no opinion, since the king has no capacity to think."

"Well, if the king himself doesn't mind, why are we making a fuss?"

"What will the international community say, with the king in that situation, yet his ministers not saying anything? The international community will say we are all idiots," said the prime minister, quite sharply.

At the moment the cabinet members were all looking at each other in confusion, Dali leapt into the middle of the room, "What kind of cabinet is this? All talking about your own interests. Talk about the situation of the people, every year afflicted by floods or forest fires. All the while exploited, deceived, or robbed or shot by armed goons. There's a judicial mafia, from the police to the prosecutors, through to the judges. Members of parliament ask for bribes to agree to the government's agenda."

However, none of the cabinet members took any notice. They just kept talking among themselves. Even though Dali thought he had been half shouting as he went around the room in the middle of the meeting. Suddenly he became conscious that he had transformed into the king's shadow. He ran home at top speed to free himself from the king's shadow. To become himself again.

As he ran, Dali said to himself: "Shadows are still shadows. Even if you're the king's shadow, still nobody pays any attention to you. The king's ministers don't care either. If people ignore the king's shadow, what do I care? But now I'm the king's shadow. Why don't they notice?"

Dali kept on talking to himself as he ran. Sometimes he asked questions, sometimes he grumbled. Sometimes he also cursed and cried out in anger. Finally, he became angry with himself, who'd wanted to disguise himself as a shadow, even if it was the king's shadow. Suddenly his running slowed, and kept getting slower. Under the shade of the mahogany trees that lined the road, he became lost in thought. As he mulled things over, it became clear to him that shadows would always be shadows. The king's shadow was still the king's shadow. When the king died, although the shadow wasn't buried, it lost its purpose. It was the shadow of the king's successor that had a role. The old king's shadow vanished. "If the king died at this moment, what would happen to me?"

As he sprinted along the road home, Dali shouted at the top of his voice, "I don't want to disappeeaar. Don't want to disappeeaar."

Arriving at his home, he found the door agape. Inside everything was black. Not a single light was on and no light entered. But he knew precisely where everything was, room by room. Even though he ran, he didn't knock into anything. Even if he had bumped into them, since he was a shadow, they wouldn't have moved, let alone been damaged. So he rushed straight into his bedroom where, when he had left earlier as the king's shadow, his body had been slumped down on the bed.

But he didn't find himself there. So he looked anxiously through all the darkened rooms. Yet, however many of the rooms he went through, however long he went on searching, he didn't find his body. In his heart of hearts, he was sure that his body, now used by the king's shadow, had gone off wandering in its tangible existence. But where had he gotten to? He searched every street and corner of the city, even looking in the slums. He didn't know how long he'd been roaming the city. Who knows how many days, how many nights.

Finally, when a feeling of hopelessness had reached a terminal state, he saw a beggar. Sitting slouched on a bench in the big park in Independence Square in the center of the city. The man was just skin and bones, shabby and pathetic. It was none other than his own body, into which the king's shadow had transformed. A part of Dali was glad that he had found his real self again. Yet, another part of him was very worried. He looked at his body that had been used by someone else. It was like shabby clothes worn by someone who didn't own them. He hesitated a moment—was it really Dali, the most popular figure of the age?

"Hey, Dali. Where did you go? I've been looking for you for days," said Dali to his body, which had been carried around by the king's shadow.

"Me? I tried to enjoy life in the real world, like a person. I thought, even though I'm a fake, it would be better than being a shadow. But I haven't enjoyed a single thing," said the king's shadow, using Dali's body. "So I was certain that I was only ever a shadow. That it was not possible for me to live as a complete person. Then I looked for you to swap places again, so I could live according to my own nature. I've been looking for you for days. Where were you?"

"I was also looking for you so that I could return to my world again," said Dali.

"It's already too late."

"Too late?"

"The king has passed away. In the grave, or in hell, the king doesn't need a shadow. How can I return to be myself, as you can become your true self again? What will become of me with your body? I won't become anything, you see?" said the king's shadow, using Dali's body. His voice sounded pitiful.

"Come on, let's swap to become our real selves again," said Dali.

"I want to. But it's not possible for me to become the king's shadow again, because the king has already passed away."

"What does that mean?"

"It's not possible. As you know, you've lost your own shadow. You'll never get your shadow back, because he prefers to live in the palace."

"What do you mean?"

"Well, that's just the nature of all shadows."

"I don't need a shadow. I only need my own body."

Dali's disputant shook his head. "You don't mean anything without your shadow."

"Now what will I become?" asked Dali the shadow.

"It's better than me, who's become a pseudo-human," said the shadow that had become Dali.

Dali, whose life's journey had once been glittering, was dumbstruck, and continued being dumbstruck, who knows until when or where.

Chatting at Lebaran

The young man was a college student. Karimi was his name. Every Eid al-Fitr, the holiday at the end of the fasting month that Indonesians call "Lebaran," he would go home to the village of his birth to be with his mother and father, in keeping with tradition. Actually, he had posed the question to himself: why go home at Lebaran? If it were to pay respects, he could just send a letter or a card or they could call each other. The question went unanswered. Going home had its own force of attraction—that is, his mother. His mother would be sad if he didn't come home. And anyway, going home for him wasn't so bad; it didn't require crossing the sea or anything.

As a member of the village, he would always follow the tradition of getting together there leading up to and just after Lebaran. Between those gatherings, he joined the events at the mosque, especially the ones at night. From age to age, there was nothing special about the mosque. The frequency of activities was higher during the fasting month, but this was because in his village there was absolutely nothing to do day or night besides religious activities.

However, there was something that left a special impression on Karimi if he came to the mosque. There were always three old men sitting on the right-hand corner of the mosque's porch, always sat in the same positions. It was as though they weren't interested in other folks, especially when they were wrapped up in talking to each other. The other people coming in and out of the mosque found them just as normal and expected as the mosque drum on the left-hand side. They were there, but no one really took much notice.

Because of their advanced age, these men were called Grandfather, or just Grandpa for short. The one with the big body was Grandpa Basa. Even his voice was big. It was unchanging, like the drone of a bass. But he rarely spoke. Normally he just let out a sound like "Yeah, yeah, yeah," or "True, true." The next one over had a body that was short and sturdy. Grandpa Kaka was his name. His voice was shrill, almost like the *keroncong* folk singers of the old days. With a voice like that, it was as though he was the only one with the right to speak. As though he was the one who had a whole cellar full of wisdom and a pile of arguments to go with it, both in opposing and in agreeing with the opinion of his conversation partners. Every time he put forward an argument, he would direct a few words towards Grandpa Basa: "Isn't that right, Basa?" or "Am I right?" or some words to that effect. The skinny one had a voice that was low and husky. People called him Grandpa Enek. When he sat, he would be cross-legged with his arms leaning on his thighs. In speaking or in listening, he rarely met the eyes of his conversation partners. He was the one who always put forward topics for them to discuss or posed questions. If it became a debate, Grandpa Basa would nod his head in the direction of the speaker, while making a noise through his nose, "Huhh, huhh, huhh."

Karimi often sat near those three old men, although he didn't quite join them. Following the conversation, there was something that made it fascinating to listen to, mostly because the topics were never the kind one finds in books or in the explanations of a preacher. "It's really not a big issue. But it can be pretty important if connected to the tenets of faith." As though thinking for a minute,

Grandpa Kaka then continued. "For example, thinking about why people circle the Ka'aba in Mecca counter-clockwise. It follows the laws of nature. Same as the rotation of the earth on its axis, the orbit of the moon around earth, and the earth around the sun. It's the same thing for a school of fish swimming around or a plant growing up the side of a tree. Even competitive runners go around the track counter-clockwise. In my opinion, anything that human beings do must follow the laws of nature. Harmonious, orderly, dialectical. If a nation violates these laws, that nation will suffer for a long time. Like our nation here."

One time, Karimi passed on their discussion about the age of the Prophet Muhammad who reached only sixty years old (by the Christian calendar). If God wanted, the age of the Prophet could have been hundreds of years. According to Grandpa Kaka, God did not want to change the laws of nature that He Himself had established. As a child of nature, the Prophet was a normal human being who became God's messenger to other normal human beings. Because of this, the Prophet Muhammad was not given miracles like other prophets. However, a prophet is a human who may not have any handicaps of any kind, either physical or mental. If he reaches a very old age, there will naturally be some handicap that he suffers from. At the very least far-sighted, hard of hearing, or toothless. He could get forgetful or senile or regress to a second childhood. "However, these days the officials in our country want to stay in their positions until the age of seventy or eighty. The president, for example. Even highly intellectual professors, with their boatloads of knowledge, are like this. Even though they know full well that this goes against the laws of nature. That's just plain greedy. They don't know their own limits. Both houses of parliament and our government are always trying to go against the laws of nature that have their own rules that are permanent and unchanging. Never changed a lick. So, by changing the laws for the needs of the moment, they ensured that legal certainty would go all topsy-turvy."

୪

Karimi once told me that the most intense debate between Grandpa Kaka and Grandpa Enek was on the tradition of celebrating Eid al-Fitr. Grandpa Enek said that the wisdom of Eid al-Fitr was in expressing gratitude because the religious community had passed through the suffering of hunger for a month. The manifestation of the joy of the people was in wearing new, fancy clothes, indulging in delicious food, visiting each other, asking forgiveness of one another. Everyone who had made a profit had to give alms to the poor equal to the cost of food for a day. "At the time of asking forgiveness from one another, no one is allowed to see themselves as higher or greater than the others. That is brotherhood in Islam."

According to Karimi, Grandpa Kaka's comments were brief. He said: "Yes. But that day full of wisdom has become muddied with traditional celebrations that are exceedingly worldly. Everything you wear has to be new, you prepare a plethora of cakes, kids set off fireworks, the rich and the poor scramble to go back to their villages, businessmen send packages to officials that cost hundreds of times what they give in alms. It is so utterly … utterly worldly."

"On the community wearing new clothes, that's to look nice, not just to show off. Going back to their villages is a priceless way of maintaining ties of kinship. Religion teaches us that we are all brothers. We have to build up relationships. This is especially true with our own mother and father. But sending packages or gifts to officials—that is truly in violation of the faith," said Grandpa Enek.

As though he didn't care about those comments, Grandpa Kaka spoke again: "When our nation was poor because it was colonized, the tradition to give new clothes to children and to prepare delicious food was a beautiful blessing. That was because the people of that time could only afford to buy clothes twice a year. It's what folks called 'Wash it—dry it—wear it.' Going home to visit parents and family, it is nothing more than still following agrarian cultural traditions. They don't yet follow a modern culture that is used to the benefits of technology. But giving such expensive packages to officials, that is the same as bribes. It's the same as violating their oath of office."

"These days it's popping up more and more. Even though preachers rail against it any chance they get. Still this negative tradition and terrible practice keep on going. It's like they're deaf," put in Grandpa Basa, at greater length than usual.

"Maybe it's the way we teach religion that has to be updated," suggested Grandpa Kaka.

"I still remember when I was a little kid," piped up Grandpa Basa again. "That was the colonial period. My father used to be a policeman. Then he worked in the public prosecutor's office. It used to be that a policeman could be appointed as a public prosecutor. When my father was in the public prosecutor's office, gifts were sent to our house one after the other. But my father would not accept a single one. Each gift was sent back to the person who sent it. That was the code of ethics in the colonial period."

Grandpa Kaka immediately echoed his thought. "That's the proof that the independence of this country actually developed the teachings that brought the nation's iniquity. You remember what I said earlier? Soekarno and Hatta, our first president and vice-president, made the country independent to raise up the level of the nation. But the leaders at the second tier took independence as a chance to take over the positions of the Dutch officials. So the people are still colonized, but now by our own people."

03

Karimi went by the house of Grandpa Basa, who actually was his grandfather. He wanted to know what interesting topics had been discussed by the three old men while Karimi hadn't been at prayers because he was away in the provincial capital.

According to his grandfather, the pressing topic had been that, according to Grandpa Kaka, Islam as a religion functioned for all humanity. This means that the actions of the Islamic community towards all of humanity—both Muslims and the non-Muslims—had to be with the same spirit of Islam. The spirit of peace. Because Islam itself means peace. "Now, as an Islamic community we are tasked with being the vice-regents of God on earth. It does not say that the objectives of this task are just for the Islamic community. As vice-regents, of course we have to treat people in accordance with the characteristics of God—the merciful and the gracious, the just and forgiving—without looking at race and religion."

But Grandpa Enek did not accept Grandpa Kaka's opinion. He said: "The goodness of God is not aimed at those who reject Him. How could we implement the same law between people who rebel against Him and people who are faithful to Him?"

Grandpa Kaka disagreed indirectly. He said, "The characteristics of God are shown by the actions of God Himself. These are the signs of God. Nature with its laws. The laws of nature demand a harmonious way of life. One aspect of the harmony of nature is that the strong have a right to live. The meaning of strength is not just physical. Physical strength is in animals. There are of course many species of weak animals that have been made extinct by the strong. But the strength of the creatures known as humans is in their wits. That is why human beings will never go extinct. Nations that are weak are just those who don't know how to use reason. Because non-Islamic nations are better able to use reason or use their brains, they are stronger than Islamic ones. That is the law of nature. So if we want to advance, well, the Islamic community has to use reason. However, we still prefer to prance around with ceremonial events and are prouder to be objects of attention than to wrack our brains."

"The place of emotions cannot be forgotten. Emotions strengthen obedience. On the other hand, rationality promotes understanding. So, emotions and rationality have to be balanced, working alongside each other. The community whose life leans more towards rationality is actually distancing itself from rituals, because rituals are seen from the perspective of their usefulness. Isn't that right, Basa?" said Grandpa Enek, as though he were asking for Grandpa Basa's help.

Then Grandpa Basa said, "Of course, I agree. Furthermore, I would say that harmonious life must be in balance. The strong defeating the weak is also a law of nature that is a sign of God. Like the animals show us, the strong prey on the weak. So smarter humans will defeat the stupid. It is true if you look at the examples of real human lifestyles. Imagine what would happen if the stupid defeated the smart. Like if the parliament was controlled by stupid people, what would happen to this country?" Grandpa Basa felt very proud because he had put forward this opinion to me. He laughed with his big voice rumbling, ha ha ha. Then Karimi asked, "What about Grandpa Kaka?"

"What did Kaka say, you mean?" Grandpa Basa asked him with a sense of surprise. A few moments later, he said, "He thinks that's it. Stupid people or weak people who want to win their fight against strong or smart people, they do it with terror. With ferocious emotions. However terrorists will never be able to win their struggle. Even if they win, then there will be terror among them, too. You know?"

ℭℬ

When I next saw Karimi, when he came back from celebrating Lebaran in his village last year, he was not as happy as he had been before. "The group of three on the veranda of the mosque has broken up. Two of them have passed away," he said mournfully.

"Who was it?" I asked.

"Grandpa Enek. Then Grandpa Kaka."

Then Karimi told me how, since the death of his two friends, Grandpa Basa didn't go to the mosque any more. He didn't even join the Eid al-Fitr prayers. He said, "It's not because he doesn't want to. It's because he cannot bend over properly to prostrate himself for prayers like you normally would. It's not a problem. I know that if it's already like this, you cannot follow the desires of your heart anymore. And anyway, folks can pray just anywhere. Like on the stones next to the creek, on the edge of a field or anywhere really so long as it is clean."

I remembered when we (me, Ajip Rosidi and Ramadhan KH) went on a trip to visit HB Jassin who was sick and housebound. Upon hearing the noon prayer call, Ajip immediately did dry ablutions (because there was no water) and did his prayers while sitting in the front seat of the car that was carrying us. Despite the fact that on a short trip like this one God gives a dispensation to combine two prayer times, like noon and afternoon prayers, it turns out that for Ajip, doing your prayers cannot be delayed. It must be on time. If you delay, who knows if there will be a new problem that comes up? I wanted to know the opinion of Grandpa Enek and Grandpa Kaka. But I never got to put this question to them.

Grandpa Basa told Karimi the story of how they three came to prefer sitting at the far end of the mosque veranda, so they would not bother people and so people would not bother them. When Grandpa Enek died, Grandpa Kaka said, "Enek has already reached the end of his road." When Grandpa Kaka also died before him,

Grandpa Basa thought that Grandpa Enek would certainly say to his melancholy friend, "I pray that he is received by God at the gates of heaven."

It seemed that Grandpa Basa knew what was in Karimi's heart. Then he said, "If Enek was the one who lived alone like I do now, I guess he would probably spend all his time in meditation and remembrance of God. But if it were Kaka living alone, he would keep doing things like he always had. He would still ponder whatever it was that passed through his mind or what he saw. His brain could not be still; it was always spinning."

So Karimi asked, "And how about you now, Grandpa?"

"There is no sadness that is as sad as that in my heart now. It started out with the three of us. All of a sudden, I am left alone. The world feels empty. So many people, but I feel like I'm alone on the train station after the train has already left," said Grandfather Basa without emotion.

I guess Karimi did not go back to his village this year for Lebaran. The village's force of attraction to pull him back is gone, because the generation he longed for is no more.

Publication History
and Translation Credits

All of the translations in this book used as their source text the versions in AA Navis, *Antologi Lengkap Cerpen* (Jakarta: Penerbit Buku Kompas, 2004). The original titles and initial publication year of each may be found in the table below.

English Title	Original Title	Year	Translator
The Collapse of Our Prayer House	Robohnya Surau Kami	1955	KWF
Maria	Maria	1956*	KWF
A Hero's Tale	Kisah Seorang Pahlawan	1956	KWF
Pride and Joy	Anak Kebanggaan	1956	KWF
Comings and Goings	Datangnya dan Perginya	1956	MGBW
A Wedding	Kawin	1957	KWF
The Two of Them	Dia Sama Dia	1958	KWF
An Interview	Sebuah Wawancara	1963	KWF
The Foreigners	Orang dari Luar Negeri	1965	MGBW
An Ideal Match	Jodoh	1975	KWF
The Water Buffalo Asks the Cart	Bertanya Kerbau kepada Pedati	1990	KWF
The Cats	Kucing	1990	MGBW
The Old Order	Orde Lama	1990	KWF
Third-Class Passenger	Penumpang Kelas Tiga	1995	KWF
Marah, Who Endured	Marah yang Marasai	1998	MGBW
Shadows	Bayang-Bayang	1999	MGBW
Chatting at Lebaran	Percakapan Lebaran	2001	KWF

KWF=Kevin W Fogg; MGBW= Matthew GB Woolgar.

*) Although *Antologi Lengkap Cerpen* lists the original publication date of "Maria" as 1956, the version included in the collection seems to have been revised at a later date, given the inclusion of a frame story about a rebellion that began in 1958.

Biographical Information

The Author

AA Navis (1924–2003) was the leading cultural and literary figure in his home province of West Sumatra during his lifetime. Although he also wrote novels, plays, non-fiction, and poetry, and engaged in government work, he is best known for his short stories. As an active participant in the Indonesian Revolution and a witness to Indonesian history from Dutch colonialism through the Japanese occupation to the conflicts and excesses of independence, Navis wrote from his own experience to challenge the culture and mentality of each era. His fiction is famous for its satirical and critical tone, while also capturing the ethos of his ethnic Minangkabau homeland and engaging with Islamic questions. The story that made his name, "The Collapse of Our Prayer House," has continued to be reprinted and taught in Indonesian schools since its first publication in 1955.

The Translators

Kevin W Fogg is the Albukhary Foundation Fellow in the History of Islam in Southeast Asia at the Oxford Centre for Islamic Studies and Islamic Centre Lecturer in the Faculty of History, University of Oxford. His historical research focuses on the position of religion in the Indonesian state after independence.

Matthew GB Woolgar is a DPhil student in the Faculty of History, University of Oxford. His research focuses on the politics of post-independence Indonesia. An earlier version of his translation "Marah, Who Endured" was longlisted for the John Dryden Translation Prize.

Translators' Acknowledgments

Both translators would like to thank the family of AA Navis, especially his widow Aksari Yasin and his daughter Gemala Ranti, who facilitated getting the whole family's permission for this translation. We also thank John McGlynn and colleagues at Lontar for their help and encouragement. Thanks also to David Workman, who read through the manuscript and helped improve its readability with his suggestions, and to Diana Darling, who made expert final edits and improvements.

Dr. Fogg would additionally like to thank Wanda Siburian for her perpetual instruction in Indonesian, including navigating some of the more tricky phrases in this book. Nelda Siburian also gets credit for improving his Indonesian, and for housing him during the bulk of this project. Anna Cumbie, Beth and Keith Fogg read over many of the stories to make sure they made sense in English. Dr. Carolyn Morningstar challenged him to take his translation to a higher literary level. Seth Setiadha provided food and distraction during a key phase of translation. Prof. Mestika Zed was very supportive of the idea of getting AA Navis to a wider readership. The Oxford Centre for Islamic Studies provided sabbatical leave in 2017 that allowed for the big push towards completion of this work. Most of all, many thanks are due to Ali Akbar Agoes, Lisa Sri Dwiyana, and their families. They not only initiated him into Minangkabau culture, fed him, housed him, and taught him enough language to get by in Padang, but they also first introduced him to the Navis family. Tarimo kasih banyak!

Mr. Woolgar would additionally like to thank Anandayu Suri Ardini, who first got him interested in AA Navis by giving him a collection of the author's short stories. That was at the end of a wonderful year spent learning Indonesian in Yogyakarta on the Indonesian Government's Darmasiwa Scholarship program, and he would like to thank the staff and student tutors at Yogyakarta State University who did a lot to improve his Indonesian during that year. He would also like to thank Sallehuddin bin Abdullah Sani ("Pak Din") and Soe Tjen Marching, who both taught him Indonesian at the School of Oriental and African Studies in London. Finally, he would like to thank Graham and Gillian Woolgar for providing shelter, support, and cups of tea during the translation and editing process.